# Lovestruck and Confused

HARINI SRINIVASAN

Om Books International

First published in 2025 by

**Om Books International**

**Corporate & Editorial Office**
A-12, Sector 64, Noida 201 301
Uttar Pradesh, India
Phone: +91 120 477 4100
Email: editorial@ombooks.com
Website: www.ombooksinternational.com

**Sales Office**
107, Ansari Road, Darya Ganj,
New Delhi 110 002, India
Phone: +91 11 4000 9000
Email: sales@ombooks.com
Website: www.ombooks.com



Disclaimer: This is a work of fiction. Names, characters, business, events and incidents are the products of the author's imagination. Any resemblance to actual persons, living or dead, or actual events is purely coincidental.



ISBN: 978-93-6395-868-5

Printed in India

10 9 8 7 6 5 4 3 2 1

**Harini Srinivasan** is the author of two historical mysteries set in ancient India, *The Curse of Anuganga* and *Shadows and Secrets: The Pataliputra Conspiracy;* the romantic comedy, *The Ex Factor*; novella, *Death at Arcade Emporia;* a children's book, *The Wizard Tales: The Adventures of Bun-Bun and His Friends* and several short stories.

A huge old Hindi movie buff, she has contributed to the recently published anthology, *The Swinging 70s: Stars, Style and Substance in Hindi Cinema*.

A former civil servant, she is an editor and a content management professional by day, and an author by night. She can be found multitasking most of the time. An aficionado of old Hindi cinema, she lives in Gurugram, India, with her family.

## Dedication

To Priyanka Sondur,

my dear friend,
for egging me on to get off my high ground and write romantic comedies! And ... for proving how bad my matchmaking skills are!

# CHAPTER 1

**March 2017, Jayanagar, Bengaluru**

**7.00 a.m.**

As one passes through Jayanagar Phase 5, an expansive vacant ground can be spotted on the right, en route to an esteemed management campus. A much-disputed space, this one is hard to miss. Amidst the high-rise apartments that have sprung up all around, this plot of land is sharply conspicuous. Just opposite the ground, among the last vestiges of a bygone era, a big old yellow-and-beige house, with its large yard, stands proud and tall.

On a particular March morning, as the rays of the sun were falling across the front yard on to the facade of the house, a young lady lay in bed, awake but eyes shut, basking in the gentle warmth, and waiting for the formal start of the day. It was the day when she was to head back to Delhi-NCR, where she worked and lived.

When Priya joined her parents for breakfast at the dining table, all packed and ready for her journey, an animated conversation about a relative was going on.

"*Enna aachi, ma?* (What happened, ma?)"

"Ranjini is coming to Bengaluru for a college trip in two weeks. Your Peripa wants her to stay here, but she wants to stay with the rest of her class," replied her father, Mr P.R. Kaushik (retd), BE MTech (IIT Madras), not looking up from the day's edition of *The Hindu*.

"Poor kid! Obviously, she will want to stay with her class. Peripa can be quite a pain!" quipped Priya. This immediately drew a stern reprimand from Sharada, her mother, even as her doting father chuckled fondly.

"What Ranjini will do, we will anyway know in a couple of days, but Priya, isn't the lease of your flat coming up for renewal?" The conversation took a turn towards the humdrum details of her existence in Delhi.

This was how the day began for Ms Priya Kaushik, our sprightly protagonist—the day she was all set to return to Delhi, where a set of unrelated events were soon to be set in motion, all of which would alter her life completely.

**Greater Kailash, New Delhi**

**The same day**

Many kilometres away, in a white three-storeyed bungalow at the corner of a bylane in Greater Kailash (GK), New Delhi, absolute mayhem was ensuing. The building was owned by Yogesh Grover, businessman and bathroom singer extraordinaire. It was certain that a situation had cropped up. No one had seen Neetu, the new help, since morning. Savitri, the head help, was naturally disapproving of the new girl. Had she run away with her boyfriend or some random driver? As most house helps are wont to do? After much cursing and searching, the missing girl was found at last—and that too in the building opposite the kothi, in Tanya baby's house! Tanya Grover, the only daughter of Yogesh and Saroj Grover, was twenty-six, unmarried and pretty much jobless.

After a small act of rebellion, Tanya had walked out and found herself a small flat in the building just opposite her parents' kothi. Much to the relief of her disapproving parents, her best friend Priya had moved in with her after her parents, the Kaushiks, had gone back to Bengaluru. Tanya, thrilled by the success of this tiny rebellion, had then decided to gain some work experience. She began assisting her cousin's wife in running her newly opened bookshop, the Sunlit Path, in the nearby S-Block market. Life was beautiful for Tanya Grover—there she was, living with her best friend, surrounded by all the luxuries and a decent job!

For the maids and other associated help, this amounted to them doing two jobs for a single pay as they ran from the main house and to the *barsaati*. However, for the wretched girl, Neetu, this was a godsend. The work was less in the barsaati and she was genuinely fond of Tanya didi and Priya didi.

After an enraged Savitri had dragged the chatty Neetu back with her, Tanya looked at the clock. So much drama and it was only seven in the morning! Neetu had sneaked in, as she did most mornings at 6.30 a.m. She used this flat as her place to cosy up to her boyfriend from Noida, Umesh, over the phone. As she cooed, she also helped Tanya and Priya get ready for the day—she made their beds, laid out their clothes and got breakfast ready. This was the only reason why the two girls didn't mind the lovers' conversation early in the morning. Priya certainly did not mind. She was anyway up most mornings by 5.30. A most annoying habit, thought Tanya, as she finally got out of bed. Glad that Priya would be back home later in the afternoon, she realized that this would be the last quiet morning in their house. Priya's cab, which ferried her to her office in Gurugram every morning, had a fixed time. Though supposed to be at their doorstep at 6.35 a.m., it was never on time. Priya always ended up spending ten minutes every morning calling the cab guys (both the driver and the transport guy at the company) to track it down. These loud phone calls, which often involved Priya barking and yelling, were Tanya's wake-up call.

The last two weeks had been very quiet. Priya was in Bengaluru, first attending a three-day conference and then spending a week or more at home. Tanya was naturally excited, not only because she had missed Priya a lot but also because she was looking forward to share everything that had happened at her end—and there was much that had happened!

The last few months at the bookshop had been defining for Tanya, and not because of her mini-rebellion and new-found independence. Waiting for customers at the Sunlit Path had instilled in her what her parents could not throughout her childhood—a love for reading! Tanya was now addicted to reading—not all books, but to be precise, just those paperbacks called Mills & Boon. She was now also a believer in true love—something that even two decades of dedicated Bollywood viewing could not bring about before. No, this was not what she wanted to tell Priya. Moreover, her new-found addiction was not completely hidden from the latter, who opined how pathetic it was that Tanya had started reading *these* books at twenty-six and not thirteen. But then that was Priya's opinion and she had an opinion on everything.

It was because of what had happened in Sunlit Path the previous Sunday that Priya's impending arrival was awaited with such bated breath. On that day, just after lunch, as the two assistants were dozing in their chairs, and Tanya was lost in a book, visualizing a dashing Italian dude betray a helpless English damsel in Florence, a hunky brown dude walked into the store. For a second, poor Tanya was dazzled and utterly spaced out. It was almost as if the Italian dude had metamorphosed into a Punjabi, Haryanvi or UP guy—as if a *Bharatiya munda* was in front of her! It was only in hindsight that she realized that her pulse had quickened, her throat had gone dry and she was left tongue-tied. Were those signs of true love entering her life?

To an observer, though, Ms Tanya Grover would have looked rather dopey, probably reeling under an after-effect of a hearty midday meal. Of course, at that particular moment, the focus of the store was on this new entrant. The sleepy assistants were up—trying to sell him the latest Amish. The man wanted something else, a book on some murders in the Mahabharata, written by an Arnab. The assistants could find no such book. Only Amish wrote on the Mahabharata, Ramayana and other such topics. Unable to reason with the sleepy assistants, the hapless customer then inquired about another volume—a long-winding title on post-colonialism by a writer with an equally long-winding name. And, the assistants obviously had no clue. Just when the now-irritated customer was about to leave, Tanya had a brainwave. She remembered the Mahabharata book. It was a book that she had seen being unpacked and dumped into a shabby pile in one of the corners. Tanya intervened and brought him the book. She also noted down the other title and assured him that she would source it for him. The relieved guy flashed her a grateful, warm, toe-curling smile, and walked away. And just like that, Tanya fell in love.

Since that day, Tanya was the first one entering the bookshop and the last one to leave, much to the surprise of Kiran. She also spent some time reading and educating herself about the latest books, authors and publishing trends, much to the surprise of everyone around her, including the two assistants. Tanya had tried to tell Priya about this new development on a couple of occasions, but somehow the time did not seem right … until this evening, when Priya would finally be back!

**Gurugram, NCR**

**The same day, late in the afternoon**

"Why didn't you call me after you landed in Delhi?" Tanya screeched on the phone. It took Priya a couple of seconds to recover.

"Hmm, I thought I did … Didn't I send you a message? I think I did … I must have. I should have. I always do."

Tanya was far from being placated. "Lady, stop having conversations with yourself in your head. It is messing with your sense of reality."

*True,* thought Priya a bit ruefully and started cooing to her best friend, who was a bit of a hyper drama queen. "Sorry, sorry, I don't know how it slipped my mind—maybe because I had to come to work, straight from the airport."

"Sorry, my foot! I have been wondering what happened. You went to office? Really? Could you not tell him that whatever it was could wait? You are on vacation!" Before Priya could mutter a yes or no the phone was disconnected.

As someone who had a fair amount of work experience, Priya should have told her boss so and not gone to work. More so, simply because KintechLearning marketed itself as being an employee-friendly set-up, which encouraged flexi-timings and offered great perks! There were posters on every floor proclaiming that KintechLearning was one of the top ten places to work at—year after year.

Priya's problem was different. Though she was twenty-six, her behaviour alternated between six and sixty-five—six when interacting with authority figures, sixty-five when lecturing Tanya and other friends. Maybe this had to do with her being an only child; or maybe with her fairly conservative upbringing—an analysis that is beyond the scope of this story.

Looking up to and seeking the approval of authority figures was definitely one of her issues. And she did look up to her boss, Sushil Sharma. A cranky, grumpy man, now in his late forties, Sharma, the head of content (e-learning and publishing), posed a threatening, intimidating figure. His long moustache, a throwback to the Sunil Dutt dacoit flicks from the 1970s Bollywood, was cultivated to terrify his young teams—both in the e-learning division and the recently started publishing division. It worked and how! Most of his team did not understand the sub-context of the moustache: the wearers of the *mooch* had hearts of gold!

"I am such an idiot; twenty-six going on six is more like it," muttered Priya as she peered into her computer screen. She had been working at KintechLearning and reporting to Sushil Sharma for two years now, since she had come back from the UK after completing her master's degree.

Sushil was glaring at the computer screen and ready to let loose a volley of expletives, when Priya walked up to his cabin to meet him.

"Priya? Are you not on vacation? I told you to call me and not come to office. But now that you are here, meet me in ten minutes," he dismissed Priya for the time being. She did not know what was worse, a hollering Sushil or a screeching Tanya, and she had to deal with both.

By evening, she was fed up! And then there was the commute back home. The commute from Gurugram to GK was bad any time of the day—and it only became worse in the evenings. What made this painful shuttle a little more bearable for Priya were her boisterous cab mates, whose loud and animated discussions made the one-and-a-half-hour ride rather enjoyable. After many close misses with the rushing traffic, Priya got home. Tanya was not yet back from the Sunlit Path when Priya let herself in. As she had finished unpacking all her stuff and was placing the different types of sambhar, rasam powders and pickles in the kitchen, Tanya walked in.

"Peeeeeeeee! I missed you," screeched Tanya, pulling Priya in a warm hug. I have so much to tell you. First you tell me, how was your trip back home? How are uncle and aunty? Ooh, aunty has sent me some Mysore pak?

Seeing the Mysore pak, Tanya remembered that there was something in her bag as well. "Arre, even I have something. Here ... the roadside vendor at the S-Block market was selling some pakoras and I had this great craving to gorge on some cheap fried food. Here you go!" she said as she switched on the TV and placed herself, pakoras and all on the sofa.

Soon, Priya joined her for a long chat. "Now tell me, what has been happ—" her gaze fell on the Hindi newspaper that was used to wrap the pakoras, and she became silent.

Tanya followed her gaze but couldn't figure out what caused Priya to pause mid-sentence.

Spreading the crumpled newspaper on the small table in front of the sofa, Tanya asked, "What happened? What are you staring at? This ad in the centre?"

Tanya stared at the advertisement to see if there was anything interesting in it. It was an innocuous center spread commercial for Ramvati Shaukeen paan masala that read: *Aaiye, apne shaandaar shauk paaliye, aur khaiye Ramvati Shaukeen paan masala.*

When Tanya looked up, Priya was still staring, almost in a daze, with her gaze strangely riveted at the advertisement.

"Priya, you eat this paan masala? Since when? *Oh baba…*"

The question broke her trance. Priya looked up horrified, "What? I don't eat any paan masala!"

"Then why are you staring at *it* like that?"

Suddenly, Priya became flustered, almost embarrassed. Saying nothing, she looked away and started fidgeting with the remote. Tanya was definitely curious. Her sensible friend did not stare at newspaper ads. There was certainly some reason. Tanya picked up the newspaper for a keen look. *Was she looking at something else in the newspaper? Something placed close to the ad, or maybe next to it? Wasn't that the premise of that new bestseller that was selling at the store? Yes, that must be it!*

With this in mind, Tanya studied all the ads next to the centre spread ad in the newspaper. Most of those were obituaries, of people young and old. Wait, what was this? This old gentleman who had departed for his heavenly abode last week had been a professor in Hindu College, the college where Priya had studied. Even if that were true, Priya should have been looking sad, not so surprised and flustered. *What if it was something worse?*

"P, baby, tell me, were you involved with this old man when in college? Did he abuse you? Did he take advantage of you?" asked a horrified Tanya.

Putting the remote down, Priya turned to her friend, with a nasty look on her face. Had Tanya gone completely mad? "I have no idea what you are blabbering about. Just stop and eat, okay?"

"No, no, what were you looking at? Whom were you staring at? This dead professor, the dead grandmother, or the shady paan masala guy? Let me look again ... Hey, the paan masala guy isn't bad ... not bad at all! High forehead, sharp nose, intense eyes ... nice. Waise, he does not look like the type who eats paan masala, though! But he must be a *shaukeen* guy! He is cute. It's okay if you were staring at him. Chalo, you carry on!"

"Uff, it was nothing. I just spaced out. Tell me about your work, na. What is new?"

Tanya fell for the bait and excitedly told Priya all about that Bharatiya dude who looked Italian and had visited the bookshop. "Priya, he had such a deep voice! When he asked me about the cost of the book, I couldn't speak. I looked straight into his deep brown, piercing eyes and all I could think of was Florence. He had to clear his throat again before I could confirm how much the book cost. And he must be so intelligent! He bought another book called *Everybody Loves a Good Drought,* besides the Mahabharata one. Imagine—who ever reads such books? He had given me a list of some other books-with intelligent-sounding names—something to do with postmodern or, what was it, post-colonialistic interpretation of something. We obviously didn't have any of those. I made that fool, Vijay, who was just standing and staring, write down the names of the books and promised the guy that I would check and try to source it. I suggested him to come back and check later in the week. What fun, na? I must get a facial before he shows up. Should I go down to Affinity tomorrow or call Komal aunty to send Renu over?"

"Oooh! So this is what you have been trying to tell me. What is this guy's name? Have you sourced these books? You see, Tanz, BD may be hot and cool too. He won't be coming to the store to simply look deep *into* your eyes."

"Arre, I am not that scatter-brained, baba. I have checked with Verma uncle. He has most of the books. He said he would send over the ones we need. Only one book remains to be located. I don't remember the name right now. Verma uncle had heard of it, though. It is by some woman named Gayatri, with two surnames—one desi and one videsi," replied Tanya.

"Ah, that must be Gayatri Chakravorty Spivak."

"Arre, waah, but how do you know?"

"I am smart and I read."

"Haan haan, you are smart, darling. *You have always been!*" laughed Tanya, as she munched the last pakora.

Getting up to clear the mess around, Tanya bent down to pick up the newspaper to dump it in the bin. Before she could even get to it, Priya picked it up and said, "You go, wash up, I will throw it away."

Newspaper in hand, Priya went inside the kitchen where, unwatched by all, she smoothened the crumpled newspaper, and took a long, long look at the paan masala guy. He was after all the man haunting her dreams! And he did not even know she existed. Worse, she had no clue who he was either.

This was a mere infatuation that began a few weeks earlier when Priya was on a draining assignment and was feeling rather stressed. In a moment of deep frustration, Priya stared out of the window from her cubicle on the second floor of her office. The KintechLearning building looked out onto a huge construction site where an emerging IT company was to set up shop. On the afternoon this assignment was due, Priya stared out of the window in a moment of deep frustration. She was sick of looking at the screen. It was afternoon and outside there were two scrawny cows grazing, a few stray dogs barking and some boys playing—besides the compound wall with all the garish posters. It was then that she saw him. No, not standing next to the compound wall, but on it! There he was, brawny and droolable, looking good on a garish poster stuck to the wall. And that was the moment when Priya's absurd infatuation commenced. Since then, every stressful moment at work was compensated for by a long, hard stare at his manly chest and his sharp nose. There were also some interesting dreams about him, but the details can be kept at bay.

It would be pertinent to say that it was only this evening that she realized the object of her infatuation was a paan-masala-chewing, endorsing man. As the full extent of her situation, the sheer absurdity, ludicrousness of it all dawned on her, she felt tortured. How could she be so silly? What was she to do now?

And Priya did not know that Tanya had seen her smoothen the newspaper and stare at the hunk's nose, chest and forehead wordlessly.

# CHAPTER 2

**The same evening**

**Somewhere in Gurugram**

The said gentleman, the one whose benign disposition graced the poster on the compound wall, the one whose eyes, lips and chest were being used to sell Ramvati Shaukeen paan masala, the ad that Priya had been gawking at, at the very moment, was standing near the window of his living room in his fifth-floor flat. He was on the phone listening to his mother, responding only with an ocassional groan or two.

"Nitin, I don't understand. Gurugram has many more apartment complexes as far as we know. Why do you insist on staying right there?"

Ma, this is a nice flat. You yourself said so. It is close to my office. Please don't start off on this again."

"Yes, it did look like a nice flat. But, my child, that was then. There have been six suicides there this year. That place is definitely haunted. You have to get out of that place."

All of thirty and an established entrepreneur, Nitin Ranganathan had moved to Gurugram two years back from The Hague and started living in Illuminati, a swanky apartment complex situated in a small lane just behind the busy, congested and happening M.G. Road in Gurugram.

Gurugram is dotted with posh complexes—apartments, high-rises and condominiums—and they promise the works. A home away from the maddening crowd, the city is equipped with gyms, swimming pools, shopping complexes and beauty parlours and greengrocers, along with having power backup and 24-hour water supply.

Like most other busy young professionals who have made their home in these apartments, Nitin was quite happy with his life in Illuminati. Round-the-clock power and water supply and Internet service—what more does a guy need? And then there was the middle-aged lady who did a decent job of cooking and cleaning. He was unsure whether she was a Bengali or a Bangladeshi—not that it would have made any difference to him. Six months back, a Japanese professional living on the tenth floor of the building had died by suicide in the children's park which was within the complex. Worse, there had been five more suicides in the same apartment complex in quick succession and all the suicide cases involved single men. Nitin's mother was convinced that the apartment complex was haunted and the resident ghosts were after the lives of single young men! And since then, Mrs Latha Ranganathan has been calling her son every other evening to convince him to move out. But Nitin Ranganathan was a stubborn young man.

And so was his mother. No sooner had he put down the phone stalling her worried pleas for another day, the phone rang again.

"Why didn't you call me back during the day, Nitin?" a sweet voice could be heard from the other end of the line.

"I have been busy! Now don't you bug me, Sowmu," growled Nitin.

"Are you home? I am coming right now. It's urgent!"

Only a few moments had passed since their conversation when the intercom buzzed to announce the arrival of Sowmya. Nitin opened the door expecting to let in his noisy elder sister and her noisier twin brats. Surprisingly, only Sowmya walked in.

"Where are the boys?"

"I left them with Bharat. I need to talk to you." Sowmya paused and looked him up and down.

"What are you doing? Checking me out?"

"Yes, yes, I have never seen you as model material, but now that you are one, I have come to check you out," quipped Sowmya, walking into the house.

"Huh, what!!!? Come again!"

"Arre, if you were planning to pose for and peddle products, you should have at least chosen some other product," continued Sowmya as she plonked herself on the couch and changed channels on the TV.

Nitin shut his eyes in an attempt to unwind, unable to figure what his sister was blabbering about. Determined not to get exasperated, he grabbed a bottle of water from the kitchen and sat next to his sister and asked, slowly, in a low voice: "Sowmya, what are you saying? I do not understand at all."

Sowmya looked at him quietly for a minute. She then pulled out a slightly crumpled Hindi newspaper from her bag and spread that out on the brown coffee table in front: "What is this?"

Nitin looked at the newspaper with disinterest, but he quickly realized the sheer horror of what had happened. There was a picture of his, shirtless, in which he was standing with his hands on his hips and a small smile playing on his lips. He was endorsing some Ramvati paan masala.

"*Aaiye, apne shaandaar shauk paaliye, aur khaiye Ramvati Shaukeen paan masala*! Isn't there any other product in the market? I mean, if you were so hell-bent on posing semi-naked, might as well have done so for a bigger, better brand!" Sowmya jeered as Nitin kept staring at the picture in shock.

A few minutes later, he squeaked, "What on earth is this? This is my picture! What am I doing in this?"

"It is you, of course! You would know what you are up to. Arre, kozhande, if you wanted to become an actor or a model, you should have told me. We would have convinced Appa. You needn't have resorted to appearing in such shady ads! What the hell were you thinking?" Sowmya added reassuringly.

"Oh fuck. I. Do. Not. Know. This is me, but I never posed for such an ad. I have no clue how my photograph landed up in this Hindi newspaper." The young man looked utterly disgusted and horrified at seeing himself peddle a paan masala. He sat back on the couch, and started changing channels on the TV, lost and flabbergasted.

"What? You know nothing about it? Oh God, this is strange! But this picture is yours, right? Or is this photoshopped?" Sowmya was now concerned about her brother; though her concern lasted for precisely two minutes. Bursting into peals of laughter, she added, "My baby brother is a celebrity ... so many girls drooling over his bare hot chest. How cool is that. There is only one hitch. All the girls are from Jhumri Telaiya!"

Needless to say, Nitin was not amused. "Will you keep quiet, and if you cannot, go home!"

Sowmya ignored her brother and continued to chuckle. After a long pause, she asked him, "What are you going to do?"

Nitin looked up at her, a little unsure and confused: "Nothing, really. God only knows how long this ad has been out there. It has not disrupted my life up until now. I think I will let it go."

"Nitin, are you not the least bit curious as to how your mugshot got on this ad? Seriously, you should demand your cut. They cannot just use your photograph without your permission! What if a Bhojpuri film-maker would like to contact you tomorrow to sign you up for his next magnum opus, *Ganga Maa Ki Kasam*? How will he get in touch with you? Wow, my brother is a minor celebrity. I must tell Amma about this." Sowmya rummaged through her purse to pull out her phone. She was suddenly excited about this new development.

Nitin, who was in no mood to listen to both his sister and mother, interjected, "Sowmya, please stop worrying about me. Why don't you go home and worry about your boys? Feed them, tuck them in bed, do whatever but stop bugging me."

"Okay. Thank you for reminding me of my boys. I will leave now. But you know what, baby, you are also my child," Sowmya said with a smile, ruffling Nitin's hair, as he shrunk back on the couch with barely disguised annoyance.

After Sowmya left, the harassed man had no clue as to what to do next and thus walked straight into his bedroom and collapsed on the bed. And the next morning, Nitin woke up fresh, fit and fine. He had decided to put that inconvenient paan masala ad as a slight aberration and move on with his life.

While Nitin may have shoved the newspaper in the dustbin, in a particular flat in GK, it still sat proudly on the kitchen top. For Priya, the night had been a rather eventful one. She did not get a wink of sleep. It is not that she was a moony teenager who would spend the night ogling at some silly newspaper ad. She had forgotten about the paan masala guy. In fact, it was YoYo Singh who had kept her awake … and Tanya and also the entire street. A noisy house party was the culprit. Adding to this cacophony were two dogs that kept barking through the night.

As a result, Priya was bleary-eyed and felt very jumpy the next morning. Neetu was late and so was Priya's office cab. To calm her anxious nerves, Priya started clearing the mess lying around in the house, and came across the crumpled newspaper lying around. Unfortunately, spotting the paan masala guy ended up putting her in a fouler mood. Priya was not used to mooning over strange men whose names she knew not and certainly not paan-masala-endorsing men despite they being fairly drool-worthy! *I am such an idiot. This fellow could be a rapist, a thug, anything! And here I am, ogling at his perfect face and body!* As she sighed, there was a loud chuckle behind her. She had got caught in the act. Tanya, who never woke up before 7.00 a.m., was not only up but had also sneaked up right behind her. "So, this is the gentleman you have been letching after since last night. He is not at all bad. Who is he? Do you know him? You did a double-take when you spotted this ad. A childhood romance? But wasn't that Karthik? Does he work in Bipin Towers, when he is not selling paan masala?

"What nonsense! Just because I look at an ad, it does not mean he is or was my crush. Stop cooking up stories using your fertile imagination." Despite putting up a brave face, Priya felt like sinking into the ground, just as Sita. Luckily, the cab driver called at that moment, "Ma'am, I have reached." A godsend indeed; Priya made her escape. "I need to leave. See you in the evening."

As soon as Priya left, Tanya grabbed the crumpled newspaper. She knew she had to look into the matter. *Hmm, I have to find out more. Priya does not ogle at anyone. Okay, there is Adam Levine and then the guy who plays Sherlock, but there has been no one else, as far as I remember. At least not since that jerk Karthik. This is strange. Or is this guy a stalker threatening my poor Pri? Eew, but he is a paan-masala-promoting guy. What if he stands in front of her office and accosts her while she is waiting for her cab, grabs her hand and says (in a very paan-masala-guy accent),* Meri ban jaao, nahin toh ...

Tanya was determined to get to the heart of this paan-masala-guy matter and help her best friend. But before that she needed to start getting ready to head to the bookshop.

**At the Sunlit Path,**

**The same day**

The GK-2 market, which was at a stone's throw from where Priya and Tanya and the Grovers lived, was rather empty during morning hours. A couple of grocery stores, sanitation stores, mobile phone stores, some banks, a decrepit-looking stationery shop–cum–Internet café dominated the market's landscape. Of course, the place was a little livelier at night—thanks to the popular eateries. During the day, it was a sleepy old market—posh at one time, now abandoned for the large, swanky malls in NCR.

The bright and colourful Sunlit Path, standing boldly next to a hip and popular café, almost felt like an outlier. One had to walk down a fleet of fifteen steep stairs to step into this haven of books. A bright multicoloured *bandhanwar,* walls adorned with small eastern trinkets, posters with interesting quotes on books and authors greeted every visitor. While the store may be small, it was always stocked with loads of books. Yes, there was that mandatory shelf full of trinkets and hip stationery items, all of which would often evoke nostalgia.

Kiran Chaddha had opened the Sunlit Path in the summer of 2014. After spending thirty years taking care of her home and hearth, she suddenly found herself with a lot of free time at hand once her daughters, Aastha and Aashna, left the nest. It was then that Kiran decided to rekindle her passion for books. During her younger days, before she was married off at nineteen, she would read anything and everything she could lay her hands on. While she could not read much after her marriage, the passion lingered. Kiran Chaddha convinced her husband Arun to invest and the Sunlit Path was eventually set up. She was very delighted when Tanya decided to work there.

On most days, Tanya was expected to get to the store between 10.00 a.m. and 10.30 a.m. Kiran would be there by that time and so would the two attendants. The morning hours were usually spent cataloguing the books, taking stock of titles and reading up on latest publishing trends. Despite her best efforts of being on time, Tanya got late that morning. It was not because she had spent quite some time staring at the newspaper, as she was worried about her friend, but because she had fallen asleep right after. By the time she woke up, it was nearly ten. As she hurriedly ran out of her house within ten minutes, she caught herself cursing the paan masala guy for entirely disrupting her routine and screwing up her morning.

As she was rushing down the stairs to the Sunlit Path, she heard Kiran yelling, "How many times do I have to explain it to you people! Why can't you just get it in one go ..."

Kiran was definitely in a bad mood. Mustering her courage and plastering a smile on her face, Tanya tentatively entered saying: "Namaste, Aunty. Sorry, I am very late."

"No problem, bachche! How are you? Here, you take over now. I have to go!" said Kiran, promptly vacating her chair behind the cash counter. Dolled up for a change, she was wearing a Ritu Kumar cobalt-blue kurta. She had just washed and let loose her long hair, which was usually put up in a tiny bun.

Tanya looked at her appreciatively and could not help blurting out, "Aunty, you are looking so good. Are you going out somewhere for lunch?"

"Haan, bachche, Pammi has organized a lunch for us sisters in the Vasant Vihar club. So I am going there. I am looking good, na?" Tanya smiled and replied in the affirmative.

Chuffed with Tanya's reply, Kiran readied herself to leave for the family lunch, which was a monthly affair, always held at the VV club, where the same food would be ordered and the same gossip rehashed (with some minor updates).

"Tanya, some Gautam Bhatt had called. He wanted to know if we now have the … what was the name … Spivak Chakraborty's book. Did he place an order for that? He also wanted to know if we have that book by Jacques Lacan … Something called *Eeecreetts*. I told him that you weren't around. He said he will either call you later or come here in the afternoon. Achcha, I am running late now," and with that, Kiran left.

Battling the fluttering butterflies in her belly and clammy hands, Tanya stood with an open mouth as she realized that she now knew the Bharatiya dude's name and that he may be visiting her that very day. Her thoughts veered from the facial appointment, which she should have already booked, and to the conversation that was to happen. "What am I supposed to talk to him about? He reads … and that too such strange books …"

"Tanya didi, are you okay?" quipped Ashok, the cheekier one of the two attendants. This prod was good enough for her to get back to work.

It was the second time in less than a week that Gautam Bhatt found himself at the Sunlit Path. The first time was entirely by accident. A disagreement with his editor had left him very irritated and as he stepped out of the office (a dark, dingy, spacious office in the second floor of one of the older buildings in the market), he was looking for somewhere to go to calm himself down. Amidst all the sanitation stores, next to the delicious-smelling café, he spotted this bright, cheerful bookshop. And that was exactly the distraction he needed. Gautam was not looking for any particular book; he wanted to just stand and stare and just be, but that pesky attendant kept asking him what he was looking for. And since he had murder on his mind (he was ready to kill both his editor as well as *this* assistant) and because the Mahabharata was one of his favourites, he uttered *The Mahabharata Murders*. Gautam Bhatt was sure that the bothersome idiot would not have heard of it and would stop troubling him.

But no, that was not what happened. Instead, the book had been located by a pretty young lady who was manning the counter. As she looked up, her sleepy eyes looked dreamy. Gautam found himself buying a couple more books and giving her some names of intellectual-sounding books (that he certainly did not wish to read) to procure. By the time Gautam left the store, his irritation with the editor had transformed into an irritation with himself! At twenty-eight, one did not buy books simply in order to speak to a girl, no matter how pretty she was.

Hence, it was with an equal amount of irritation and nervousness that Gautam Bhatt, a journalist by profession and a novelist-in-the-making, found himself again in front of the bookshop. Over the past few days, since the first trip, Gautam had forgotten all about the books and the girl from the store. He didn't remember about the books until that morning, when one of the people he had to interview for a breaking-news story he was working on suggested the delectable café next to the bookshop as the meeting place. When he called the store, he was all set to cancel the order, but then he heard the name Tanya and remembered the dreamy-eyed girl. He ended up staying mum. As he entered the Sunlit Path once again, he decided to keep his irrational self in check and was determined to simply pick up the books he had placed an order for and leave.

Tanya was busy reprimanding the pesky assistant for failing to complete a simple task without mistakes. She looked up at Gautam quizzically. Despite her fascination, she could not recognize him (something that would later mortify her a lot—how could one be fascinated by someone and not recognize him when he is right in front of one!). Gautam politely introduced himself and reminded her about the books. The puzzled expression in her eyes was immediately replaced by the same dreamy look as before—much to Gautam's chagrin.

Several minutes later, just when he was about to give her another list of books, he gathered whatever little composure he had and blurted out. "Look, I do not know why I am doing this. I do not require these books or the ones that I told you about. I would like to get to know you better. Will you have a cup of coffee with me after work one of these days? My name is Gautam Bhatt and I am a journalist."

"You are asking me out on a date? You do not even know my name!"

"Your name is Tanya. I know that. I am asking you out on a date. Will you come?"

"Yes, I think I will … When?"

"Tomorrow evening, in the café next door, at six."

"Okay. You really do not want any more books?"

Gautam shook his head, gave Tanya the most warm, toe-curling, smile and walked out, relieved that he could still manage to talk to women. And before she could realize, Tanya Grover was in love with this good-looking man in less than a week.

"Everything has a reason. Maybe this is why I started working at the Sunlit Path; I had to meet Gautam Bhatt," Tanya was swooning while talking to Priya later that evening.

"How could you just agree to go on a date with him? Do you know anything at all about him? Who is this Gautam

Bhatt? He could be anyone. Seriously, Tanya. And now you are busy weaving your dreams of happily-ever-after with him. Really?

"Come on, at least my dreams are about and with someone I have met—unlike some people who are busy mooning over paan-masala-spewing near-naked men," retorted Tanya.

Ignoring the comment and focusing on her Sudoku puzzle, Priya said, "Do whatever. I have warned you. If you wish, I will come and sit in the café tomorrow and look out for you."

The conversation soon petered off, with Priya concentrating on a particularly hard Sudoku puzzle while Tanya surfed channels, dreaming about her date the next day. Gautam Bhatt, on the other hand, was finishing a story that he had to submit the very next morning.

# CHAPTER 3

Over the next three weeks, time passed by rapidly, especially for Tanya. Having fallen in love quicker than one could bat an eyelid, she was now in the throes of the initial days of courtship and life was definitely on the upswing. It was a heady phase and things were speeding up at breakneck pace. Gautam had met Tanya's parents and also introduced her to his own family based in Dehradun. It was starting to seem like wedding bells were just around the corner. Gautam, who had been focused on his professional pursuits, was now spending more and more time with Tanya either at her place or in the bookshop. Priya had also given her wholehearted approval after meeting Gautam, and to Tanya's utter delight, they had hit it off very well.

It had also been very busy time for Priya. The months from March to April were always busy for her, with client meetings, fresh targets, goalposts and several new projects coming her way. This meant that Sushil Sharma was more hyper than ever and in a perpetual bad temper. In evenings, she would be kept occupied by the sudden, whirlwind romance in Tanya's life. Back home in Bengaluru, her mother and grandmother had taken to sharing essential details (photos, biodata and horoscopes) of good, eligible boys over email, Facebook, Messenger and WhatsApp. And strangely, Priya wasn't bugged. She was thankful for all these constant distractions, all of which had relegated the paan masala dude to complete oblivion.

After the last few weeks, on a particular bright sunny morning, the second floor of KintechLearning was abuzz with rumours. From being an exclusive e-learning shop, KintechLearning had moved to educational publishing (both print and electronic) over the last two years. While not as successful as the e-learning division, the publishing division had been slowly making inroads into the market. A townhall for reporting the year-end fiscal results was scheduled later in the day. Promotions, demotions and transfers would follow such sessions. This year, there were added expectations regarding some big announcement about the publishing division. It was also rumoured that Sushil Sharma was up for a transfer. After all, he had irked everyone, inlcuding his boss, subordinates and even clients.

The corporate accounts e-learning division was on tenterhooks, as their boss was crankier than usual and they themselves were oscillating between hope and apprehension. Sushil Sharma was not agitated because of his rumoured demotion and transfer. It was due to an account with a telecom major that he had been managing that was coming up for renewal. A dreaded meeting was awaited, as the team handling the account had goofed up. The accounts director at the telecom major, an erstwhile batchmate of Sharma's, had called him the previous evening and indicated that this may be a roadblock to the renewal of the account. Sharma, acting upon that, had restructured the core team as a firefighting measure first thing that morning. A formal call with the client's entire team confirmed that this measure was certainly not going to be enough. Desperate measures called for desperate times; Sushil Sharma was determined not to let the renewal fall through.

"It's boss on the intercom! Oh, no!" Priya groaned as she picked up the phone.

"Come to my office, Priya, now!" The morning was turning out to be busier than expected.

"Yes, sir. You called for me."

"Priya, did you see the email I sent you?"

"The one informing me of my reassigment to that telecom account, sir?"

"Ah good, read up as much as you can. The documentation is on Sharepoint. Just get a sense of the project. The renewal is to come through in any way. We are going to Mumbai this afternoon. Have asked the travel desk to book the tickets. Now get going."

Later that afternoon, Priya was at a cafe overlooking a crowded bookshop at the Delhi airport. As she sipped a cup of coffee, waiting for her boss to join her, she spotted *him*. It was the man from the newspaper advertisement, in flesh and blood, all of six feet, beef and brawn!

Nattily clad in jeans and T-shirt, he was browsing through some magazines in the bookshop across the café. *He can read! He also wears clothes!* Priya's heart skipped a beat. As she was staring curiously, she saw two warring boys, not more than four feet tall, run up to the guy and demand his complete attention and help in sorting their fight. Priya's mouth fell open. The clothed paan masala dude was a dad—a married man with twin boys.

"Hey, Priya! There you are. Why did you not pick up your phone? Let me grab a coffee, and then we can go to the gate." Sushil Sharma had shown up at that very moment.

Priya could feel her heart shatter into pieces as she witnessed her pathetic nascent attachment with a paan masala model come to an equally pathetic end! "Oh, I did not hear it ring amdist all the noise here. Sorry," Priya managed to respond with a nod and a forced smile.

***

In the bookshop, the five-year-old twins Advait and Vivek Ramamohan were kicking up more of a fuss than normal while their indulgent maternal uncle pampered them. Nitin Ranganathan was in a happy, relaxed space. A close friend of the Ranganathan siblings was getting married in Mumbai, and Nitin was travelling with his sister and his bratty nephews to attend the same. After the wedding, the siblings were to head to Bengaluru to meet the parents. He was looking forward to this much-needed break. The past few months had been very busy for him, as his business had started looking up. His software firm, Parity Global, had bagged several lucrative new contracts, and the team had also expanded in Gurugram. He and his partner were even contemplating getting an office space in Bengaluru.

Meanwhile, Sushil had reappeared with a takeaway coffee cup in hand. "I am going to the bookshop. Coming? Or will you head to the gate?"

Poor Priya was in a tight spot. While she did not want to go to the bookshop and ogle at her married crush and his kids, at the same time she also wanted to. She wondered whether his wife was around and how she looked.

"Coming, sir," muttered Priya, giving in to her impulse.

As they entered the store, Sushil spotted someone he knew at the cash counter. Instead of browsing through the magazines, he called out: "Nitin, how are you? Good to meet you here! Where are you off to?"

It was thus a surreal moment when Nitin Ranganathan turned around and walked up to them and greeted Sushil Sharma. "Hello, Mr Sharma, good to meet you here indeed. Off to Mumbai and Bengaluru, but will be back in time for our meeting on the sixth."

To Priya's utter shock, there *he* was! The paan masala guy standing in front of her, and worse, her scary boss knew him! In order to not come across as a complete gaping idiot and to avoid any conversation, Priya had in the meantime turned to browsing through some magazines from the stand, wishing that she could simply disappear—either sink into the ground or evaporate into thin air.

However, that was not to be. Sushil, suave as ever, turned to her and said, "Priya, meet Nitin Ranganathan. He heads Parity Global and will soon be collaborating with us on the digitization project. Nitin, this is Priya Kaushik. She is our content development manager. We too are off to Mumbai." Introductions were followed by small talk over weather and other inconsequential topics. Of course, it was Sushil who did most of the talking, with Nitin contributing just a wee bit. Priya had managed to pull off her most reassured and reserved exterior, something that could come across as intimidating, as she had been told once. Just when Priya thought she could not carry on with this facade, the boisterous twins accompanied by their equally boisterous mother made an appearance.

"Nitin, look what I found. Amma would love it," said Sowmya as she excitedly walked towards this party. The boys were just behind her, engrossed in some imaginary game and discussion. As Sowmya was being introduced, the boys' discussion took a heated turn and she had to excuse herself to intervene. In the ongoing mayhem, Priya missed Sowmya's introduction as Nitin's sister. She was engrossed in observing Sowmya and her obvious affection for the man in front of her. With this conversation abruptly getting over, Sushil and Priya soon made their way to the gate followed by Nitin, Sowmya and the kids.

In a busy airport, that too on a weekday, Priya Kaushik unexpectedly met the man who had been haunting her dreams. The meeting left her fluctuating between elation, dejection, irritation and simple curiosity to know more about this married paan masala model, who, as it turned out, also owned a software firm. Thankfully for her, the plane ride to Mumbai was a rather uneventful one. Seated right in the front in the first row, Priya was far away from Nitin and his family. Sushil was all charged up and wanted to discuss the strategy for the upcoming client meeting. He brought Priya up to speed and so they spent most of the time on the flight preparing for the meeting which was scheduled for the next morning. This was just the diversion Priya needed. By the time they landed in Mumbai, she was feeling much better.

On the other hand, in row 23, Nitin had been subjected to a rather intense interrogation. "Nitin, who was that girl? Do you know her? I think she is very pretty, what do you think?" Always on the lookout for a potential bride for her younger brother, Sowmya had taken a liking to Priya instantaneously. She was rather disappointed that the meeting had been too short, all thanks to her twin brats. So once she had settled the kids and given them their books to read and toys to play with, she focused on extracting more information from her brother. Nitin was fully aware that the meeting with Sushil and his pretty colleague had made an impact on his snoopy, bossy sister. What he did not and would not mention ever is that he had found Priya Kaushik attractive. Were he to mention to his sister about every woman he found attractive, he would be in deep trouble. So, he patiently waited for his sister to raise the topic and when this question was raised, he replied, in a pointedly disinterested manner: "No, I do not know her. Met her for the first time."

Unnoticed by the siblings, a gentleman seated in the window seat in the same row was staring at Nitin with much interest. Sowmya noticed that and whispered to her brother in Tamil, "Looks like today you'll be meeting all acquaintances. That guy by the window, the one with those big goggles, has been staring at you. Do you know him?" Curious to know whether the man Sowmya was referring to was actually an acquaintance, Nitin turned towards the window seat.

Devesh Tiwari Nirala was a poet at heart and a film-maker by profession, even though his poetry had won him more fame than his films. There had been more takers for his collection of poems—in both Hindi and Bhojpuri—but there were no takers for his movies, as both his Bhojpuri releases had tanked and badly at that. Nirala-ji had spent the past six months doing a lot of soul-searching, which had resulted in another collection of poems that had been picked up by a local publishing house. When it came to making another movie, it had seemed as if there was no light at the end of the tunnel. In a bid to connect to his audiences, he had travelled extensively. While he was still looking for a suitable story, he seemed to have found and finalized the cast (well, a part of it). Ranjeeta Singh, a twenty-year-old college student from Kota, was his latest find; he had already signed a contract with her. As for his hero, Nirala-ji found him in Hisar where he had gone to reflect upon the larger meaning of life and what future had in store for him.

There was just one tiny, little hitch—his hero was splattered upon the compound wall of a cowshed and hence couldn't be signed on! Nirala-ji had spotted the famous Ramvati paan masala ad and had decided that the model featuring in it would be his hero! He was sure this man with the fair Ranjeeta would end his *saade-saati* in the Bhojpuri film industry.

The initial soul-searching expedition soon transformed into a frantic hero-searching journey: Nirala-ji made a concerted effort to locate the incredibly attractive man. Unfortunately, no one knew who he was—neither did the people at Raj Group, the company that made the paan masala, nor the photographer from whom the photograph had been sourced. In fact, Nirala-ji had almost given up hope of being able to trace his hero.

The lost hope and suppressed dreams resurfaced the moment he saw Nitin walk up to the same row and sit next to him. Nirala-ji was observing Nitin from a directorial point of view to see which camera angle would enhance his handsome side profile and which angle would make him appear sexier! Nirala-ji was a bit concerned that, in person, Nitin appeared a little too nerdy. Such thoughts were flooding his mind till the point Nitin, nudged by Sowmya, turned to talk to him.

"Hello, do I know you?" asked Nitin, worried that he might have forgotten the man's face.

"Oh! Not quite! You do not know me, but I definitely know you," beamed Nirala-ji, way too excited that the hero had initiated the conversation. It was definitely a sign from above! Soon, an animated conversation followed.

"Oh, so you say you know me?" repeated Nitin, looking rather unsure.

"Sir, please do tell us how you know him." Needless to say, Sowmya was now a part of this conversation.

"Sir-ji, I have been looking everywhere for you for so many days now. In fact, I am a big fan!" continued Nirala-ji.

Naturally this proclamation left Nitin shell-shocked, and for a moment, even Sowmya was stumped. She regained her composure and asked, "Sir, you say you are his fan? But what has he exactly done?"

Nirala-ji, using this godsend opportunity to revive his non-existent movie career, waxed eloquent about Nitin and his charms. "Your smile! Your body! Looking at the ad, one wouldn't even think that you are a new model. You have no idea how talented you are. I have identified the hidden talent that lies within you, which is why I have been looking for you for the past four months! May I please have your good name? Myself Devesh Tiwari Nirala from Kanpur."

This impassioned speech by Nirala-ji was received with varying reactions. The curiosity of the passengers seated in the nearby rows was triggered. "Was this guy a model, an actor? Have we seen him before? He looks decent but not sure about his model looks." The twins had stopped playing their game and were wondering why everyone was talking about their uncle. Had he done something very naughty and got caught? That didn't seem to be the case, as their mother was not at all angry or upset.

"His body! His smile! His talent!" chortling with laughter, Sowmya looked at her brother with renewed interest.

Nitin, not too happy at being the centre of such attention, managed to respond to the overeager Nirala-ji, "Sorry, Nirala-ji, I do not think that I am the person you are looking for. I am certainly not a model or an actor." Seeing Nirala-ji's face fall at this unequivocal rejection, Nitin put his hand forward to shake the man's hand and added, "My name is Nitin Ranganathan and I am a software professional. Sorry, I am not the person."

Nirala-ji, quickly recovering from this initial rebuff, grasped Nitin's hand, "No, no, please don't say this. You are the same person. One shouldn't be so modest now, Nitin-ji." He promptly proceeded to bring out the Ramvati paan masala ad from his bag. Gazing at it with unfazed fascination, he said, "Have a look. Isn't this you! What a body … here, show this to your Mrs too." To make his point doubly clear, he thrust the ad into Nitin's hands.

At being addressed as Nitin's 'Mrs', Sowmya burst out laughing, "No, no, I am not his Mrs. In fact, I am on the lookout for his Mrs-to-be. Please let me also have a look, Nirala-ji … Well, this is definitely Nitin. Nitin, you have been doing such great work and you haven't even told us! Very bad." Taking the conversation even further, she added, "Namaste, Nirala-ji, *my* name is Sowmya, I am his elder sister. You can tell me why have you been looking for Nitin all this time."

Since this was just the encouraging opening Nirala-ji was waiting for, he promptly launched into a lengthy monologue about his childhood, his family, his dreams, successes and failures. Finally, ten minutes into this monologue, he spoke about his new film, the next magnum opus in Bhojpuri cinema, for which he had been looking for Nitin. He declared that Nitin and only Nitin could do justice to the complex role, bringing to life the various facets of the multidimensional character, being the talented, good-looking man he was!

Halfway through this monologue, Nitin had lost interest and was in fact thankful that his sister was keeping this crazy film-maker company. However, when he realized that the filmmaker wanted to cast him in his next movie, he was flabbergasted. Shaking his head, with an incredulous expression on his face, Nitin slowly but firmly said, "Nirala-ji, thank you very much. But no, I am not a hero or a model. Yes, this is my photo; but please try to understand, I am not interested in your offer."

Seeing Nirala's downcast face, Sowmya sweetly intervened and asked him for his details. "Dekhiye, this was completely unexpected and no less than a surprise. Nitin anyway never makes a decision in a jiffy. Please give him some time to think about it. Meanwhile, you can give me your card, and we will get back to you."

Thankfully for Nitin, before Sowmya could make any more promises, the plane began its descent towards Mumbai airport. In the ensuing rush that followed, it seemed to Nitin as if the farcical meeting had come to a close and they had finally lost sight of Nirala-ji. But that was not the case. They spotted him, or rather he spotted them, just as they were walking to the baggage carousel. Further pleasantries and such exchanges continued, mostly between Nirala-ji and Sowmya. Since Nitin was anyway a mute spectator in this conversation, he had been relegated to managing the twins. Funnily, it was this image—of Nitin playing with and managing the twins—that was to sit firmly in Priya's mind, for this is what she saw when she left the airport.

# CHAPTER 4

The flight from Delhi to Mumbai had been completely packed, lending to a chaotic situation near the baggage carousel. Everyone was obviously in a hurry. Nitin was in a hurry to escape from the deadly clutches of Nirala-ji; Sowmya was in a hurry to get out of the airport, as the twins were beginning to get cranky. As Nirala-ji was picking up his luggage, ruminating merrily about the twists and turns he could include in his magnum opus, now that he had found his hero, a gentleman bumped into him. Nirala-ji fell on the floor, with his suitcase lying open next to him. As he struggled to stand up, expecting a profuse apology, to his abhorrence, the uncouth gentleman had simply vanished. Instead, a young lady who had been standing next to him offered him her assistance. By the time Nirala-ji got up, Sowmya had also hurriedly come to his rescue.

*"Hum toh bas khade thhe, bade tuchchh aadmi thhe woh! Humein giraake khud bhaag gaye,"* Nirala-ji complained. His

wounded pride was soon gratified by the commiserations proffered by Sowmya and the young lady. And balance was restored. Goodbyes and farewells exchanged, Nirala-ji finally set out to his sister's house in Kandivali.

"Good riddance! Seriously, Sowmya, did you have to speak so much with that film-maker? Nirala-ji this and Nirala-ji that!"

"Really?! All I did was talk to a strange film-maker; you are the one in shady ads."

"Nitin mama, are you going to be an actor?" squealed the twins, who had had a stuffy flight, after being shushed repeatedly by their mother and uncle.

"Not at all. Why don't we just hurry to Vijji paati's home? Have you forgotten our plans? Srinath mama is waiting for us. Do you boys remember him?" Nitin distracted the excited twins, while glaring at his sister.

"You and I need to talk later, Nitin Ranganathan," retorted his elder sister, as the party left the airport.

The Mumbai leg of their trip was to pass without much excitement at least as far as Nitin was concerned. Nitin spent most of his time playing with and babysitting his nephews and catching up with some close friends who were also in Mumbai for the said wedding. The twins were being pampered and doted upon by their maternal grandparents, who had flown down to Mumbai, and their uncle whom they hero-worshipped. With much time on hand and no husband to deal with (read: manage), Sowmya was having a blast. Shopping, spending hours at the spa and, add to that, catching up with

Asma and Medha, her closest friends from schooldays who were now in Mumbai, life was definitely looking interesting.

As the three women sat at a cafe gazing at a beautiful sunset one day, silently reflecting upon their lives, a stocky, portly middle-aged man looking rather strange in a blue outfit topped with a cap of the same colour, came up to them and said, "Asma-ji, do you have a minute to spare? *Zaroori baat karni hai*."

Asma looked a bit uncomfortable when she excused herself from the table hurriedly. "Medha, who was he? Do you know him?" asked Sowmya, as her interest was certainly piqued.

"Na re. Don't know who this man is. Actually, we hardly meet. It is because you are here that we are meeting. Asma has a busy family life, so she doesn't have much time to meet up. Let us ask her once she comes back."

Their curiosity immediately turned into concern on seeing Asma in tears when she returned.

"What happened? Are you okay?"

"No, I am certainly not. Salim is a cheat, a two-timing jerk!" The hitherto frivolous, chatty conversation turned into a sombre heart-to-heart talk. Asma told them, as they listened with barely disguised anger about the philandering ways of Salim, her husband. Asma recounted how she had put up with this but now she neither had the strength nor the inclination to remain in the relationship. What Asma had heard and seen thirty minutes back was the proverbial last straw. The stocky gentleman, the one with the strange get-up, was a detective. Sanjay Dhamija, detective sans pareil, who was also a Dev Anand aficionado, founded and ran Sharp Eye Detective Agency. Of course, his reputation stemmed purely from his agency's success rate in tracking down errant spouses or finding just the exact cause that could break a marriage. The excellent services offered by Sharp Eye Detective Agency in this particular domain was what made Sanjay Dhamija such a widely sought-after detective in the elite Delhi-NCR circles and off late amdist South Mumbai groups too.

Asma had got to know of him via her neighbour, who had personally vouched for Dhamija and his detective skills. And there, barely fifteen days after bagging the assignment, he had proved himself again. He had the necessary proof of Salim's infidelity—proof that Asma could use to get rid of her cheating spouse!

Asma's monologue got Sowmya thinking. *This Dhamija fellow could be helpful in finding out how Nitin's face landed in that offensive ad.* Was Nitin lying to her? Was he actually moonlighting as a model? Maybe, the poor boy always wanted to become an actor and since he couldn't, he was now pursuing his childhood dream by becoming a model. As these barragc of thoughts kept surfacing in her mind, Sowmya was convinced that Dhamija could be of use. When Asma had calmed down a bit, with the help of her friends' support and the situation was restored to a semblance of normality, Sowmya asked gently. "Asma, umm, I was wondering, could you please put me in touch with Mr Dhamija? There is a small problem I am dealing with."

"What! Do you think Bharat is cheating on you? Oh God, no, he comes across as a decent guy," blurted Medha, totally in shock.

"No, oh no, please! It's not Bharat. It's Nitin. I am not sure what he is up to," said Sowmya emphatically.

The recent extreme feminist utterances about men and marriage were promptly forgotten as the women now shifted to discussing about the glowing benefits of marriage and how it would cure Nitin of all his misguided fantasies. It was unanimously decided that Nitin must and should get married soon. Asma, in spite of her own marital crisis, along with Medha assured Sowmya that they would extend their help. On this promising, uplifting note, the coffee date of the three friends came to an end.

During the entire course of the wedding over the next few days, Sowmya was obsessed with the paan masala advertisement and the subsequent movie offer and other possible shenanigans Nitin might have been up to. She had contacted and spoken to Sanjay Dhamija and plans had been made already to meet in Delhi a couple of weeks later. But first, the issue had to be brought up and duly discussed at their home in Bengaluru. Appa and Amma had no clue about the whole sordid affair. Bharat, who was also in town for the wedding, had to be told—not about Nitin's saga (which he knew about) but about the WhatsApp forwards (only of the philosophical and poetic kind) Nirala-ji had been sending her almost every other hour. This had caused her much amusement, but Nitin had been horrified. And he had brought it up during a conversation with Bharat and Sowmya.

"Seriously, that is some crazy guy, and she has gone and given her number to him. How very stupid! She doesn't listen to me. Maybe she will listen to you," Nitin complained to Bharat.

"Ha ha, you should know better. What am I to say? Sowmu, I hope you aren't meeting this crazy man in a bid to make your brother a film star."

"Really?! Now you too, Bharat? Nitin goes and gets into trouble and I get blamed for wanting to get him out. No, I am not meeting him. Nirala-ji is seriously quite helpless ... he is anyway being so nice to me only because he wants Nitin ... as a hero I mean. Don't you worry, if I receive even one obscene forward or message from him, he shall be blocked.

"Fine then, Nitin, how on earth did you land up in the ad? I was shocked when Sowmu showed me the newspaper. Where did they get your shirtless pic? Was it at a club? Did you even know you were being clicked?"

"Oh God, no, no, Bharat. As I have told Sowmu every single day since then, I really do not know how and where this picture was clicked. This is highly embarrassing. Amma and Appa don't know yet, but I need to tell them soon. I do not even know where all to check to have the ad pulled off," Nitin cribbed to his brother-in-law.

"Arre, we will hopefully come to know all about it in the next couple of weeks. I promise you guys. I will find a solution by then. All we need to do first is break the news to Amma and Appa. Let's do that once we reach Bengaluru!"

Sowmya's confident and calm assurances piqued her husband's curiosity. "What are you up to, Sowmu?" asked Bharat, rather sternly. He knew his wife and her machinations a bit too well.

"Nothing at all. I am just trying to figure this out using my sources. You just relax."

"Look, whatever it is, please do not get into trouble," he continued. Sowmya purposely chose that moment to attend on one of the twins. Kids, after all, come in handy during such sticky situations with the spouse.

Once the wedding in Mumbai was over, Bharat returned to Gurugram while Sowmya and Nitin proceeded to Malleshwaram, Bengaluru. Even though Nitin's parents and sister complained often about how unlivable this city had become, for Nitin, it was home—Malleshwaram in particular. Despite all the recent developments that had led to the cribbing about the deterioration of their beloved city, Bengaluru was any day better than dusty, uncouth Gurugram.

For Nitin, the moment he stepped into the city, there was an unspeakable joy, an indescribable elation that filled his soul. He felt happy and at peace and tended to turn a bit poetic. Nitin was a bit of a romantic and a closet poet. Sowmya had known about his poetry-writing spree since he was a teenager and in the throes of a rather acute crush he had on one of his classmates—a fairly vacuous but pretty girl. But once that time passed by, Nitin stopped writing poems. However, unknown to Sowmya, he had recently resumed his old hobby—though this time, there wasn't a particular girl to whom these were being dedicated to, at least not at the moment. Once he landed in his hometown, he felt optimistic and upbeat, all the worry about the random happenings in his life flew out of the window.

"Good Lord, the traffic just becomes worse every time. It is so warm and it's just April. Uff, Addy, Vivek, stop moving. Look at that blue car. Why don't you count the number of cars? Let's see who counts 100 cars first, okay? No, Nitin mama is not in the competition. Nitin mama and I have to talk."

"No, we don't, Sowmya. Vivek, look at that red car. That's the tenth car ..."

"Nitin, instead of counting cars, think of how we can tell Amma and Appa about your latest adventure. How their kozhande is now a renowned paan masala model and is about to make a mark as the next Bhojpuri superstar!" All this travel was beginning to get on Sowmya's nerves—especially at a time when there was this big mystery that was begging to be solved. Truth be told, since she had heard of Dhamija, she had been contemplating a future as a detective herself.

"Calm down, Sowmu. I spoke to Vikas yesterday. He is checking up on it and will let us know what legal recourse is available in this situation. People cannot use my picture—photoshopped or otherwise—without my consent. Now stop fretting. Do you know what plans Amma and Appa have for the next few days? I think we should go to Melkote and Srirangapatna, if we can. It has been ages."

"Oh, yes, we should go there for sure. Maybe God will listen to my and Amma's prayers, and you may just get married soon."

"Look there, that's such a substandard paan masala ad. I look so much better than this man, don't I, Sowmya?" Unfortunately, Nitin's desperate attempt to distract his sister from the much-abhorred topic of matrimony did not work.

The discussion on the topic did not end with their cab ride from the airport, it came up again at home. This time, it was his mother doing the prodding. She wanted to understand her son's hesitations. A frail, sweet lady in her sixties, Latha Ranganathan, unlike her daughter, was not a very interfering person by nature. Latha mami, as she was fondly called, was content teaching Carnatic music to some children in the neighbourhood, spending time in her garden and visiting the Sri Krishna temple on 11th Cross daily. A cancer diagnosis, six months back, had pushed her to worry about Nitin's marriage and Sowmya's general state of excitability. Given Nitin was so quiet and so undemanding, she was not sure whether it was the bad break-up with his college sweetheart that was responsible for his lack of any interest in marriage now. Sowmya had pooh-poohed the possible reason when they had discussed about it. "Amma, Nitin is fine. I don't even think he was that serious about her. He hardly wrote any poems when they were dating." Latha could not see any reason in this half-baked theory cooked up by her overenthusiastic daughter. Being a woman who was geared towards finding solutions to problems, she checked with her sisters regarding eligible girls in their community, and started sending pictures that she received with the respective horoscopes and biodata to Nitin. This trip to Bengaluru had been anticipated by both

Latha and Ranganathan. Latha had decided to find out the core reason behind Nitin's aversion to marriage. Ranganathan, on the other hand, wanted to spend time with his children and grandkids. He tried to dissuade Latha from raising the 'm' word, but when did his wife or any of his kids ever listen to him!

One day, after a sumptuous meal, fully satiated and rested, the family was playing a game of Uno, when the topic was brought up again—and not too subtly. "Nitin, what are your plans? I would like to see you married before I die."

Nitin winced at this direct emotional assault and immediately protested at the unfairness of it all. "Amma, it is not that I do not want to get married. I just haven't met anyone I would like to marry. And those pictures you keep sending me every other day feel like an intrusion into my privacy. I haven't even looked at them. But for your sake, I will, from now on. Just stop this drama, though."

Sowmya, surprised at this immediate capitulation, asked, "Arre, Nitin, how come, when I try this, it never works?" All she got as a reply was a dirty scowl from Nitin.

"Because you probably try this every day," interjected her highly amused father.

Relieved at this satisfactory answer, Latha proceeded gently, dabbing her eyes (a subtle masterstroke appreciated highly by Sowmya), "You know, if there is someone you have in mind, let us know. I just want you to be happy, kozhande."

"Ma, I do not have a girlfriend right now, definitely not one I am serious about. I will let you know when I would like to get married. However, if it makes you people happy, please go ahead and find me a suitable match," explained an embarrassed Nitin. He really had no wish to upset his mother, especially not when she was recovering from the dreaded cancer.

"Oh wow! You actually spoke more than two sentences. Nitin, maybe if you continue like this, you will soon find *the one*. I shall make sure of that," remarked his sister, which resulted in a well-aimed cushion landing up on her head.

"And maybe you can continue and tell Amma and Appa about all the exciting things you have been up to," said Sowmya, snarkily throwing the cushion right back at Nitin. However, her aim was awry and it sparked a mini-cushion war in which the twins also participated enthusiastically—Vivek on Sowmya's side and Advait on Nitin's! Just the digression Nitin was in need of at the moment. He was tired being the subject of intense scrutiny by his family.

"But wait, what did Sowmu mean when she said that you have been up to some exciting things. What is going on?" Latha, who had caught on to the mention of "exciting things" in Sowmya's taunt, was not the one to let this pass without seeking an explanation.

"Yes, Amma, our Nitin is now a well-known model across the Hindi heartland. He is much sought-after for naked paan masala ads!" Sowmya, who had been waiting for just this opening, butted in.

"What?!"

Seeing the shock on her parents' faces, she told them about how she had spotted that ad accidentally in a newspaper in which spinach came wrapped at her home. "Imagine my shock, Amma, when Sarla pointed it out and asked, *'Yeh aapke bhai model kabse ban gaye?'* I did not know what to say! It was our Nitin and that too endorsing some cheap brand of paan masala. Uff. Too much."

The entire account was heard with pin-drop silence. Ranganathan and Latha were dumbstruck, as they just could not understand the whole story and they looked at their son with a bewildred expression.

"Amma, Sowmu is, as usual, exaggerating. Yes, my mugshot has landed up in some lurid ad. But I do not know how. I certainly haven't become a model!" The harried Nitin repeated slowly what he had been saying all along. He really had no clue.

"You do not know about this picture at all? How can they just shoot you when you are scantily clothed and not even let you know about it? This really does not make sense," said Ranganathan, looking rather pensive.

"Yes, Appa. It definitely does not make sense. That's what I have been saying. How can Nitin not know that his picture was being taken ... unless he was drugged or drunk or downright stoned," interjected Sowmya, much to Nitin's irritation.

"No! I was not drugged or stoned or drunk or unconscious. Sowmya, hold your imagination in check!"

# CHAPTER 5

**Meanwhile in Delhi**

After Priya left for work one of these mornings, Neetu asked Tanya: "Didi, has Priya didi been doing okay? She has been seeming off lately."

"Everything's fine ... it must be the office work. She must be exhausted due to it, it's not that she is sad. Have the washed clothes come back from ironing?" Tanya deftly changed the topic. But Neetu's comment had left its mark. *Was Priya really sad? What could have happened? How could I have not known?* Was Tanya so lost in her new-found bliss that she had not noticed her best friend's sadness? Worried, she started observing Priya closely for the next few days. As per her observation, she certainly seemed subdued and was even spending more hours at work.

"Priya has become much quieter. And I do not know why. Even Neetu was commenting about this change. What should I do?" she asked Gautam one evening.

"Umm, well, why should that even be a problem? Priya is probably just tired. Does she not travel all the way to Gurugram? Tanya, it could be due to anything. Maybe more work? Or maybe her boss is terrorizing her more than before. Really, you should stop," Gautam quipped, unable to understand or even recognize Tanya's extent of worry.

This did not stop Tanya from further contemplation. There had to be a stronger reason for her friend's mellow mood, and now it was her duty to find out the possible reason behind it. She started spending more time at home with her, paying close attention to her.

Gautam was right. The reason behind Priya's changed demeanour was work-related. Ever since she had come back from Mumbai, her workload had shot up. The meeting in Mumbai had been fairly successful. Sushil and Priya were able to convince the miffed telecom client to renew their contract. But now Priya was handling two major accounts—one being a European oil-and-gas major, and the other being the miffed telecom giant. And to make matters worse, Sushil had informed Priya that she would additionally be handling a new digitization project. Ever since Sushil's promotion had come through, he was handling two portfolios, one in the e-learning division and the other in the new publishing division. All her so-called indifference, as fathomed by Tanya and Neetu, was more because she felt overworked and underpaid.

However, something had changed since the Mumbai visit. Previously, the poster on the compound outside her window at work used to be a stress-buster. Ogling at the pleasing photo and the droolable chest of the small-time pan-chewing poster boy used to help alleviate whatever stress she faced. But that was not the case anymore. These days, the sight of the said poster boy proved to be plain disconcerting, for it reminded her of the man behind the image—a decent and well-mannered man, one who was *also* a doting father. That was certainly not okay. Now all she could think was him playing with his kids or feeding them or taking them to school—and that is not how she wanted to picture the man of her dreams.

After many oblique and unsuccessful attempts to get to the bottom of the matter, Tanya gave up and asked Priya directly, "Are you depressed? You look so sad these days. What's the matter? Uncle and Aunty are fine? Are they forcing you to get married? Is someone troubling you at work?"

"What? Huh, no, why would I be depressed? I am just stressed—there is so much work. Can you believe it? Tanu, I am handling three goddamn mega projects, all with demanding clients who are barely satisfied. And they don't even pay me well. All I get here are peanuts! Damn! This stress is for sure depressing me," replied Priya.

"Oh, it's just work then? I thought it was something else, something more important. Maybe Uncle and Aunty ..."

"Just work, Tanya?! What can be more important than that?" scoffed Priya, going back to what she was doing—surfing channels and looking for something inane to watch.

Tanya, slightly dissatisfied but now more at peace, picked up the scholarly book that Gautam had gifted her. Each time she'd pick up the tome, she'd get lost in his thoughts, daydreaming about him. Getting past even two pages was seemingly impossible. But since she needed to do something, preferably read (her new hobby), she picked up a Hindi magazine left behind by Neetu. As she flipped through its pages, she came across the now-familiar paan masala ad, this time in colour and gloss, and the man looked really good! "Priya, look, that ad we saw in the newspaper. This model is really nice. Wonder who he is and where he is. He hasn't starred in any more ads, na," exclaimed Tanya.

Torn between curiosity and irritation, Priya snapped, "Tanya, stop ogling at stupid ads. There are so many models. Why would I remember this particular one? It's getting late and I am sleepy. Goodnight."

While recounting this episode to Gautam the next day, Tanya recalled finer nuances such as Priya's pallor, her fidgeting and irritability. "You know, baby, Priya got so irritated when I showed her that ad. I wonder why?"

"Look, Tanu, you are letting your imagination run wild. Poor Priya. On top of all her work stress, you are now quizzing her about a random ad and model. Really, you should stop reading all those idiotic romances. How far have you got through *In Search of Lost Time*?"

Tanya listened to the lecture that followed, quietly, as her mind ran in a thousand directions trying to find a solution to the problem at hand. Nothing was to dissuade her from finding out what was bothering her dearest friend and helping her.

The next morning, Tanya's suspicions were confirmed, or so she thought. Priya had left, as usual at 6.45 a.m., complaining about the commute, prodding Tanya to wake up. As she sat sipping a cup of ginger tea, listening to Neetu's stories from the *bada ghar*, Savitri paid a visit. She had come to retrieve the latest edition of *Grihshobha* (the very magazine that had caused Priya so much consternation the previous night). Strangely, the magazine was nowhere to be found. *"Arre, Neetu, maine toh issi mez pe rakha thha. Tumne uthaya toh nahin?"*

The newspaper was soon traced in Priya's bedroom, next to her pillow! *"Didi, mil gaya. Priya didi shayad raat mein padh rahi thhi. Unko Hindi padhna aata hai?"*

*"Chalo achcha hua mil gaya, jaake de do phir Savitri ko,"* Tanya replied slowly, keeping her face completely expressionless. It seemed to her that her brainy, sensible friend had fallen for some *sadak-chhap* model. And something had to be done about it, no matter what Priya claimed or what Gautam advised.

Tanya went about her day, praying and looking for some direction as to how to proceed further. And as they say, seek and you shall find, she did find a solution, that too through Gautam. Gautam Bhatt, when not wooing Tanya, worked as a journalist. His latest story was on a drug and prostitution racket in one of the upmarket areas in Delhi. While he did manage to collect enough material, he was still on the lookout for some explosive information that would guarantee him a scoop. This came up in a conversation with Tanya when he met her for a quick lunch at the Sunlit Path.

"Tanya, I am meeting an actual detective today. Since you have a very fertile imagination, imagining all sorts of things, I thought this would interest you."

"Detective? Wow. What does he look like? James Bond type?"

"Bah, you should meet him. Forty-plus uncle type, a little plum, and thinks he is Dev Anand. He knows everyone and everything. Very highly recommended!"

"What are you getting him to investigate?"

"He has this huge network of informers ... and I need some information."

"Achcha, what is his name and does he have an office and all?"

"Sanjay Dhamija. Speak of the devil—I have no idea why he is calling. Will be right back."

A Google search of the name provided the necessary information. By evening, Tanya had a confirmed appointment with Sanjay Dhamija at Sharp Eye Detective Agency. She was to meet him two weeks later.

Situated on the fifth floor of an artificial limb centre, near the famous spinal injury hospital in south-west Delhi, Sharp Eye Detective Agency functioned out of a two-room office and had a three-member team. The detective agency was set up seven years back, when Sanjay Dhamija, then a second engineer in the merchant navy, had a sudden brainwave. He chucked his job and found an office space. It was no less than a big risk. As he was foregoing the handsome pay, his decision had been questioned by his wife and other family members. His foresight seemed to have paid off pretty well. Considered one of the brightest and most capable detectives in Delhi-NCR, his office saw a steady stream of clients wanting to hire the company's services. The cases were mostly the same—men and women suspecting their spouses of infidelity and expecting proof to either repudiate or substantiate this belief. There had been other types of cases too. Along with his own network from school, college and family, Dhamija had cultivated his own source bank, the *khabris*, who worked with local police and goons alike. All in all, his career as a detective had taken off much better than expected.

That day was no different. Dhamija had attended to several visitors, comprising prospective and current clients, all expecting a quick solution to their woes. "*Kitne din lagenge aapko?*" was a constant question.

Among the prospective clients visiting Dhamija that morning was Sowmya Bharat, desperate to find out more about the infamous guy from the paan masala ad. Sowmya had been trying to fix an appointment with Dhamija for three days now. And each time, the appointment had been cancelled at the last minute by Dhamija's secretary, Sanvi. The excuse was always the same, "Boss is busy with an urgent matter and cannot meet you." The fourth time, Sowmya decided to take matters in her own hand and barged into the agency, without an appointment, first thing that morning. Though the office timings on the website and the board said

9.30 a.m. to 6.00 p.m., the sleepy office came to life only by 10.30 a.m. When Sowmya entered the office, there was Sanvi, Dhamija's sister-in-law, also the receptionist and secretary, and Hari and Sanjeev, the two office boys. Dhamija had a story of his own behind why he decided to hire Hari and Sanjeev. A major Hindi movie buff, he was excited when he heard their names the first time. After Dev Anand, if there was a hero he liked, it was Sanjeev Kumar, whose birth name was Harihar Jethalal Jariwala! So when Sanjeev and Hari wanted work, they were immediately hired as office boys. While they did nothing in the office, they were very helpful when it came to scouting for information and tailing someone.

Coming back to the meeting between Sowmya and Dhamija, it was certainly less explosive than what the former had expected.

"Dhamija-ji, I saw you in Mumbai. You helped my friend Asma. I got your reference from her. I need your help."

"Oh, okay, I don't remember seeing you. But how may I help you? Is your husband cheating on you? Are you cheating on him? Do you want to divorce him? Do you need some proof to prove he is a scumbag, so that you can divorce him?"

Stunned by this volley of questions, Sowmya was silent for a minute. "No, not at all. My husband is a good partner, and no, I do not want a divorce. This is regarding someone else."

"This someone else wants a divorce? Is his wife cheating on him?" intervened a bored Dhamija, as Sowmya rummaged her purse to take out the newspaper.

"No, no, he is not even married. In fact, everyone wants him to get married. Can you help?"

"Ma'am, this is a detective agency, not a matrimonial one!"

"Oh, sorry, I am so distracted. The problem is that—he is my brother," said Sowmya pointing to the ad.

"*Isme problem kya hai?* He is very good-looking and is a model. Is he not successful?"

"Dhamija-ji, *wohi toh problem hai*. He is not a model. In fact, he himself does not know how he landed here in this ad. I want you to find out."

"He does not know how he appeared in this ad—and that too in this state—semi-naked? How can that be?"

"That is why I have come to you. You pride yourself on being a great detective. So, please help me figure out this mystery."

"Look, ma'am, your brother may be lying to you. Maybe he did this ad, because he needed some money, maybe for drugs or alcohol or something. And then he was embarrassed when you got to know about it. Now, it will even get tough for him to get married. Maybe that is why he has lied to you."

"Hmm, maybe you are right, Dhamija-ji. But I would still like to believe my chhota bhai. Why don't you take this case up, and help me find the truth? If this is a photoshopped image, you can find out who did it, and if my brother is lying, you find out why he is lying. Either way, *aap hi ka case hai.* If you want, I can help you at every stage—in this case as well as others, on weekdays," reasoned Sowmya.

Dhamija looked at the lady in front of him. He liked her. She was persuasive and to the point. Plus, he was sick and tired of tailing errant, cheating spouses.

"Chaliye, okay ma'am. I will take up this case. And what do you mean by you can help me?"

"Dhamija-ji, you are a reputed detective. But do you have a proper team? No. There's just this secretary-cum-receptionist, and these two office boys. What is your job after all—chasing people, talking to your sources, extracting information from them. I too am good at all this. On top of it, I am a married woman, and a mother. If I would be the one asking questions, wouldn't there be higher chances of getting answers? At least, I can look more credible and trustworthy than your khabris. So if you wish, I can join you as your associate, work weekday mornings when my kids are at school, and help you with some of your cases in Gurugram. But this is optional. For now, more importantly, I want you to take up my brother's case."

This prepared and rather rational answer had Dhamija convinced. He was known for his risk-taking, decision-making abilities. He just made his next decision. He accepted Sowmya's proposal and recruited her as his associate in Gurugram. He assured her that the financials would be worked out the next day. Also, not known to waste any time, Dhamija assigned her a case to work on, only if she was eager to start even before the formal contract signing. Sowmya indicated that she would love to. A gentleman from Gurugram who had approached Dhamija the previous week suspected his wife of cheating on him and wanted her tailed and every moment reported. Dhamija asked Sowmya to follow up on the case and report any findings to him.

This sudden turn of events had left Sowmya surprised. Truth be told, she hadn't gone there looking for any kind of association. Her agenda had been simple: she just wanted to know how did Nitin's face land up in that ad? (She was sure that the ad was photoshopped; her nerdy younger brother did not have such a Herculean body!) But when she came to that tiny office and saw the rush after her arrival, she figured that she could help out here. Even when she had put that proposal forward, she certainly hadn't thought he would accept it. What was to be even more of a surprise or rather a shock was the name of the client. Anurag and Sharmila Batra lived in the same building as Sowmya, and their kids went to the same school as her sons. She couldn't believe that Anurag was suspecting Sharmila to be cheating on him, especially when, to Sowmya, Anurag was the one who came across as the philanderer. Tailing Sharmila was definitely easier and more feasible than tailing completely unknown people in shady parts of Gurugram.

# CHAPTER 6

**Two weeks later...**

The paan masala model loomed large, poster-size, in the minds of both Tanya and Priya over the next two weeks, for very different reasons. Tanya was sure of the kind of dirt the detective would dig out about the said model—he may just be a fading Bhojpuri porn star addicted to drugs and alcohol who had to now act in such lowbrow ads; or he may be an out-of-work model who has now fallen under the clutches of some local Bhojpuri goon. Whatever the scenario, she had to help her friend and be there for her. There was also the added guilt of keeping this from Gautam, fearing that it may throw a spanner in the works and hamper their new relationship.

One day, she blurted out this planned upcoming meeting and all her suspicions to him over a cosy cup of coffee. To her relief, Gautam did not fly off the handle. He simply shook his head and said, "Tanya, too many romantic books have addled your brain. What can I say? Do you want me to come with you when you meet Sanjay Dhamija?"

"Oh, will you? So sweet of you," said Tanya, throwing herself in his arms, absolutely delighted at this support.

While Tanya's vivid imagination had the paan masala model don so many avatars, Priya was grappling with a different challenge on the same day. Barely fifteen minutes after she got to the office that morning, she heard Sushil's voice echo on the intercom. "Priya, we need to touch base on the digitization project. Come now." Suppressing her irritation, which invariably stemmed up from such unplanned meetings, she walked up to Sushil's room, to see the object of her fantasy, the said paan masala model-cum-married man, sitting there.

"Aah, Priya, come on in, meet Nitin, Nitin Ranganathan. Nitin, this is Priya, our content development manager."

"Hello, Priya, thanks, Sushil. We had briefly met that day at the airport," replied Nitin, extending a hand to the now-very-spaced-out Priya.

Thankfully, just then, another gentleman walked in causing much commotion. "Sushil, Priya, this is Vinod Vaidyanathan, my partner and co-founder at Parity Global. Vinod, this is Sushil Sharma. He heads content here and this is Priya, the content development manager with whom we would be working," introduced Nitin.

"Thanks, Nitin. Hello, Sushil, good to meet you. And you too, Priya. How are you doing? How are uncle and aunty?"

"I am fine and so are they, Vinod. Good to see you here," replied Priya, much to the surprise of Nitin and Sushil.

Introductions over, the discussion was centred on the modalities of the digitization project that Parity Global was to handle for KintechLearning. A team from Parity Global would work out of the KintechLearning office space three days a week. Nitin also mentioned that he himself would be present at least two days a week and would be the point of contact should there be any issue. By the time the meeting was over, Priya's erstwhile stress-busting poster boy was now posing to be a big stress factor at work, for she was now absolutely attracted to this married, multifaceted gentleman, one who ran a firm besides being a model!

The first week of the project went by without any major gaffe on Priya's part. KintechLearning had entered into a partnership with a consortium of leading Indian universities and it had expressed interest in a searchable database and analytics tool. Besides the proprietary content of KintechLearning, such as its own print course material, e-learning and Moodle-assisted course content, the searchable content would also include books and journals in the respective libraries. KintechLearning had also acquired over 200 journals, all of which were to be digitized and fed into a searchable database and analytics platform before the end of the year. It was a big project by any standard, both for KintechLearning and Parity Global. The latter had been hired to not only digitize these journals and any other material that would need to be added but also programme and develop the database and analytical tools. The young team from Parity Global (for the first phase) included a lively content analyst, Urvashi, and two experienced programmers, Abhishek and Anuj. This was a golden opportunity for them to prove their skills and worth, and they were enthusiastic and raring to go. With office expansion and a couple of other big projects at hand, Nitin came in only once that week for the project kick-off. From KintechLearning, besides Priya, there was the other content development manager, Vishal Ganotra, and a couple of junior business and content analysts. Priya had upcoming deliverables in both her other e-learning projects. As delivery manager, handling two high-profile accounts, her focus was now on getting the courses up and running. Since it appeared that the schedule may not be met, she was already preparing the scene for firefighting. After the initial internal meeting with KintechLearning, she had spoken to Sushil about this and it was then that he decided to rope in Vishal for the project. However, he had made it clear that she would be the one to manage the client, a consortium of several universities, fulfil their expectations and maintain vendor relations, while Vishal would handle the day-to-day execution. She had no complaints with this arrangement. It suited them both fine. By the end of the week, Priya had no time at all to dwell upon her idiotic infatuation or related apprehensions.

When Nitin Ranganathan and Vinod Vaidyanathan started Parity Global out of Nitin's Gurugram apartment, they had no idea that it would become as big as it had. They got their first few projects with the help of an extensive alumni network, and slowly capitalized on it. And now, besides a small office in ritzy DLF Square, they had also recently set up a small office in the BTM Layout in Bengaluru. Vinod, who had been looking to move to Bengaluru to be closer to his parents, was grateful for the opportunity. He had flown to Delhi earlier that week for a meeting with a potential client. And on Nitin's suggestion, he joined him for the Kintech meeting. As they met over the weekend to take stock of all impending projects and things that needed to be done, the first work week at the Kintech project also came up.

"I hardly got any time this week to go and spend time at the Kintech office. Urvashi and Anuj mentioned that they were getting a grip on the requirements. Plan to go and meet the content development manager on Monday. And, Urvashi mentioned that there is another CDM who had been assigned to this project, other than your friend, Priya. She is pretty."

"Oh, Priya's parents too live in Jayanagar, just next to Appa and Amma. She is pretty for sure. I didn't think she is your type!" replied Vinod.

"A girl doesn't need to be my type for me to appreciate her attractiveness. You sound like Sowmya, Vinod!"

"How is Sowmya? Haven't seen her in a while. Kids keeping her busy?"

"Come to think of it, my pesky sister hasn't been bothering me either. It's been a whole week, busy or not, she usually drops by or calls," mused Nitin, suddenly concerned.

"Why don't you call Sowmya? Maybe she and the family can join us for dinner?" suggested Vinod as Nitin got busy locating his phone to call his sister.

"Sowmya said she would come over later," Nitin mentioned after the rather short call. "You know, I wonder if she is okay, the conversation was rather too short. This is not normal."

The conversation was short because he had called at an inopportune moment, at a time when Sowmya was busy trying to eavesdrop. Seated with fellow mothers of Belvedere Park, as they watched their kids play an enthusiastic game of soccer, her entire focus was on a conversation taking place in the row behind her, where Sharmila Batra was spelling out her day to a neighbour.

Since her meeting with Dhamija-ji the other day, Sowmya had become more neighbourly, making frequent appearances at the park, club and parlour—anywhere she could bump into Sharmila and formally befriend her. Not that she had been not-so-neighbourly before. She, after all, had a close circle of friends within the condominium—mainly from her yoga and pilates class—ladies with whom she would occasionally grab a cup of coffee. Sharmila was not among these groups. Sowmya was now often seen waving enthusiastically at all neighbours, especially the ones who had been spotted with Sharmila. While this approach had not yielded much result yet, she had been lucky to unearth another source of information. Sowmya's cook, an old Bengali lady who had been with them for the past three years, had decided to go back to Medinipur for a wedding and had deputed her niece to come in her place. Sowmya, initially not too happy with the idea, warmed up to it the moment she found out that the said niece also worked at Sharmila's house. Using this as an appropriate opportunity to cultivate some sort of a working relationship, Sowmya contacted Sharmila (via WhatsApp) and conducted a background check. The cook was slow but good. Sowmya thanked Sharmila profusely and also sought her advice regarding the school their kids went to. She tried fixing up a meeting. A tenuous bond was thus established, giving Sowmya a slight reprieve from the frenzied waving and beaming. After several conversations with Sharmila and the gossipy replacement cook (about the *neeche-wali memsaab*), Sowmya had a handle on the unsuspecting woman's schedule.

Despite these efforts, much to Sowmya's dissatisfaction, nothing was found amiss. Sharmila Batra came across as a typical, married Gurugram mum, her interests matching with many other women who were active members of an upscale FB group. Sowmya eavesdropped on Sharmila's conversations; tailed the lady around Gurugram and Delhi daily but still couldn't get a single proof or any sign of infidelity. This strengthened her belief in the idea that most men are idiots—do they not get it? Why would any woman sabotage her completely perfect life with an enviable lifestyle (aided by a fairly efficient support staff, surrounded by many friends to gossip and chit-chat with) by getting involved with some other man for fifteen (if at all) minutes of pleasure?

She shared her concerns with Dhamija: "Dekhiye, Dhamija-ji, Mr Batra is way off the mark. There has been a misunderstanding. Sharmila Batra doesn't seem to be having an affair—after all, she has such a content life!"

"Ma'am, her husband is clear that their marriage has been rather strained. They aren't even on talking terms … I wonder how she looks happy …"

"That's what the problem is, Dhamija-ji. Mr Batra feels that just because he is not on talking terms, his wife is sad. And he is assuming that if she continues to remain happy in spite of his not talking to her, then she must be having an affair! Seriously? Who does he think he is? Arre, I tell you, she is happy because he is not talking to her. He is a very boring man. I have been following her. She is content—her kids are good, her parents and sisters live close by and then there are all those classes and exhibitions she attends. There is no affair going on!"

"Mr Batra says that she has been spending too much time on phone and WhatsApp."

"So? Doesn't make sense at all. Arre, it's not that she is a schoolkid or a college-going girl that she'd keep talking to her boyfriend on her phone? Had she really been hiding an affair, there would have been some proof. Sorry. Please inform Mr Batra that he should stop worrying about his wife's fidelity and if he wants to get back to talking terms, he is the one who should make an effort …"

Notwithstanding these daily update calls, Sowmya also decided to meet Dhamija in person. It is always good to meet one's work colleagues face-to-face. She fixed an appointment in a week's time. Her mother was expected to land in Delhi later that week, and hence the week after that would be the perfect time.

However, to not lose her practice and touch, Sowmya continued to tail Sharmila and that was what she was doing when Nitin had called. The reason for her ending the call quickly was only that she had started enjoying eavesdropping. One got to hear so many interesting things that happened in other people's lives.

She would recount some of these stories while having dinner with her family, and Nitin and Vinod. "Sowmya, how do you come to know about these things? Gosh, you have turned into Meera aunty!" quipped an astonished Nitin, who certainly did not know of her sleuthing activities.

"Who is Meera aunty?" Bharat wanted to know, as he burst into a chuckle.

"The local gossip-monger in Malleshwaram. She has always known each and everything that went on in every house on 15th cross."

"Very funny, Nitin. I am sure Sowmya just finds people interesting," Vinod pitched in Sowmya's favour.

"Indeed. She finds people so interesting that she eavesdrops on their conversations—not at all like Meera aunty," countered Bharat.

Sowmya, irritated by now, turned the conversation back to Nitin's infamous ad, of which Vinod had no clue.

"Look at our famous model, Vinod. Does he not look so hot?"

"Aha, this is classic. The paan masala ad dude! How much did you get paid for this exhibition of self?" Vinod asked, bewildered.

"Thank you very much, sis. Don't ask me, Vinod. I have no idea how my face has landed on this ad. It is just one of those strange things for which there doesn't seem to be an explanation," rued Nitin.

"You look rather nice, I must say ... I must show this to pretty Priya and see what she thinks," chuckled Vinod.

"Who is pretty Priya?" Sowmya butted in immediately.

"A colleague whom I met a few days back and whom Vinod knows well. My mistake was in commenting that I found her pretty. But let me add, she is not my type. So please, you need not start your matchmaking now. Gosh, Sowmu, you're so becoming Meera aunty. Bharat, how do you put up with this lady day in and day out?" retorted Nitin, clearly indicating that he wanted that conversation to end.

Sowmya had found another bit of information to chew on and wasn't going to let it go. She made up her mind to pursue this Priya track separately with Vinod, after checking with her mother.

Latha Ranganathan, far from being interfering in general, had become concerned about Nitin even more so since she had heard about the infamous ad. She was anxious that his lonely, bachelorhood existence, with no other interest besides work, had perhaps started affecting his mental stability—probably the reason why he had started appearing in risqué ads. *Arre, why doesn't he resume his quizzing or playing the mridangam as he used to?* With all sorts of worries in her mind, she decided to go and stay at her daughter's place for a while, on the pretext of helping her out. Her son-in-law was a good man who wouldn't mind her presence at all and the twins were absolute darlings. That way, she knew she could keep an eye on her son without being too obvious and maybe figure out what was wrong with him. Her husband, who did not approve of the plan, told her point-blank that he was not travelling to Delhi-NCR in summer, and certainly not going to interfere in Nitin's life. Latha made it clear to him that the welfare of her son was more important than the wrath of the sun, and proceeded to book her tickets. In the last week of April, Latha Ranganathan landed in Gurugram, determined to sort out her son's woes.

# CHAPTER 7

On a particularly hot May morning, Dhamija felt the heat more acutely—it was as if he was running amok the streets of Delhi, trying to solve cases that he could not make any sense of. One of these unsolved tricky cases was that of the Batra's, which he had outsourced to his new associate. He wondered whether he made a wrong decision the other day. Though, to him it was certain that of all his quick and impulsive decisions, the one to outsource the case to the woman had to be the craziest. He did not even know who she was. *Didn't even get her background check done. One sight of a confident, outspoken lady, and I went mum. Now she says there was no case to begin with—and that Anurag Batra is a mad man to suspect his wife. Arre, how can I go and tell Batra that? Bhai, he has given such a hefty advance.* As if that was not bothersome enough, Dhamija was also fed up of the wild-goose chase Sowmya had set him on, pushing him to find how that boy's face got printed in that ad. *Bhai, the young man might have wanted to model or act, and so he did. Conservative family got to know, so now he probably is feigning innocence. Yeh bhi koi case hai?! Uff!* Though his mind was swamped with such thoughts, he had assigned Hari, one of those two good-for-nothing dolts, to find out more on the case. He was hoping that Hari would find out something and be back in office on time that day, for that Sowmya lady was to meet him to discuss the cases.

Besides meeting Sowmya, Dhamija had one more meeting scheduled. He had wanted to cancel or postpone it. But Sanvi had told him that it had been fixed long time back, and moreover, it was the new girlfriend of that somewhat famous journalist whom he knew. Some Tanya, it seemed. He was now looking forward to his meeting with both the ladies.

The meeting with Sowmya went exactly as he thought it would—stormy and inconclusive.

"How can you say that, ma'am? What proof do you have? Just because you cannot prove that the lady is cheating on her husband, you cannot go about accusing the poor man. On what basis!"

"Dhamija ji, have you heard of gut feeling? Instinct? From the day I have seen him, I have intuitively felt that he is a cheat. Now he suspects his poor wife, whose only fault—if it can be called that—is that she is a spendthrift. But then again, she has the money, so she spends. Yes, she spends hours at the malls, but that is to check out the latest styles in stores, not to meet some hidden paramour. How can he just assume she is cheating on him? *Aap unko bol do, dimaag check kara le apna. Aap nahin bolenge toh main bol doongi, lift mein dikhe toh,"* replied the indignant lady.

"Look, ma'am. Okay, you couldn't find the proof that Mr Batra wanted us to find. That is okay, we can explain that. But I cannot accuse him of cheating because my associate feels he is. Got it?"

"Okay, whatever. You don't believe me, that's alright. I will just get you proof one of these days and then you can tell him. By the way, what happened to my brother's case? Have you been able to find out anything?"

"I had sent Hari to find out more. He should be back today. Will get back to you soon."

"Hari? That idiot who can't serve a cup of tea without spilling! Pah! If you keep such people at work, your business will sink one day. Chaliye, I am off now."

On the way out, quite irritatued with Dhamija, Sowmya was lost in her own thoughts and she almost bumped into a young girl who was walking in.

"Good morning, Mr Dhamija. I suppose Gautam would have mentioned that I require some assistance. I am Tanya Grover, his girlfriend."

"Haan ji, good morning ji, please sit. Now, how may I be of any help?"

Tanya delved into the matter right away and produced the edition of *Grihshobha* that she was carrying with herself and opened to the page of the ad and pointed: "Yeh dekhiye. I want information about this man."

Dhamija could not believe his eyes. He rubbed them and looked again. "This photo? This semi-naked, the Ramvati Shaukeen paan masala man?"

Tanya stared at him, trying to figure out why this middle-aged gentleman, supposedly a detective par excellence, was squawking like a duck. Had he not seen a shirtless, bare-chested man before? "You are right, this is the person. I want to know who he is, and what does he do besides selling Ramwati paan masala? Can you do this much? I will pay of course ..."

Dhamija, now slightly recovered, quipped, "Haan, haan, I can find out and tell you all about him. But what I do not understand is why are you so interested in him. Gautam is in fact a good guy, much better than him."

"Oh ho, Mr Dhamija, just because I want to know who he is does not mean I am romantically interested. There can be many more reasons. *Aap bas pata kijiye aur bataiye.*"

Dhamija's innate curiosity and suspicion was now triggered. *Who was this young man? Why were so many women interested in finding about him and his activities? Was he really Sowmya's brother? The two hardly look like brother and sister. What if, in reality, he is actually her husband? God knows what goes on in those upscale condominiums in Gurugram. Too much paisa and too little morals. Maybe she hired me to keep an eye on her man and report his dealings. Pata nahin, what young men these days are up to. They hardly bother about their kids and family. Uff! And who knows—this guy might be stalking this poor girl Tanya and harassing her. And that's why Gautam had sent Tanya to me—to seek my help. I should help her. I will handle this case myself and not depend on that idiot Hari to find out more about him.*

With such sympathetic thoughts towards both Sowmya and Tanya, Dhamija heartily assured Tanya that he would find out all that needed to be found out and report to her as soon as possible. Tanya came out of the meeting feeling more assured than before, even though midway through the meeting, she had started double-guessing Gautam's judgement. If this bumbling middle-aged man was a super-sleuth, she may as well as be the queen of England.

Tanya's propensity of walking straight into people, things and doors on a regular basis ensured that this time she bumped into Hari. He was a thin, quiet guy who definitely did not want to work, which is why this office suited him just fine. With not much to do, he sat watching movies and songs on his new phone for most of the day. Therefore, he wasn't too happy about being given an additional assignment. He did not understand why boss wanted him to track down the makers of some ad. But then he figured it had something to do with that bossy Sowmya madam. *Must be her husband,* he thought. *Once married, what was a woman to do other than run her husband's life and track the poor man's whereabouts.* With such misgivings about the whole assignment, Hari had spent the week tracking the origins of the ad but to no avail. No one, absolutely no one, knew who the photographer was. He even got Sanvi to speak with the publicity manager at Raj Group in English.

All Hari could verify from him was that somebody had brought in the photograph, and they used it as they liked the face. Moreover, somebody from the film industry was also looking for the same guy a few weeks back. Hari was to call the publicity manager the next day to retrieve the name of the man who was looking for the paan masala guy.

Just when he was on his way to relay to Dhamija whatever little information he had collected, he found himself on the ground, sprawled, with his things lying scattered. A young lady, looking completely shamefaced, was apologizing to him for having not seen him. "Sorry, I am so sorry. Are you okay?" Just when he thought happily that he was to be helped up by a pretty woman, she instead of picking him up, bent down and picked up that ad. "Do you … do you know this man? Is he your friend? Why are you carrying around this ad?"

Hari blinked as he realized that the pretty girl was more interested in this stupid man's picture than in helping him. In an indignant tone, he replied, "Not at all, ma'am. This man is not my friend. Will you now step aside? I need to get up."

"I am sorry but do you know this man? Anything? His work or address? Is there anything you know about him?"

Looking at her eager face, Hari, now up on his feet, almost felt sorry for this girl. He decided to clear all confusions and said, "You must have often seen or maybe met Sowmya ma'am, who comes here. She was here this morning as well. This guy is her husband. She gave this ad to us to find out when he went and became a model."

Yes, Tanya remembered that woman—she had bumped into her earlier the same day. She remembered because Sanvi had addressed her as Sowmya ma'am. "Well, do you know anything else about him?"

"His name is Nitin. Also, Sowmya ma'am has two kids—so he too would, and look, he is still posing for such cheap advertisements. Ram Ram!" replied Hari rather officiously, indicating he had to enter Dhamija's office, especially because Dhamija was now yelling his name.

Tanya quickly thanked Hari and left the office in a state of shock, her mind abuzz with lots of thought. She was now worried for poor Priya, for the dude she was lusting after was not only married, his poor wife was also sending detectives to track him down. Her favourite Mills and Boon do offer such infinite wisdom—good girls fall for horrid, depraved men. Tanya thanked her stars for Gautam and his goodness. But now that she had fallen for a good man, did it mean that she was horrid? What does the gospel say about this? Tanya put this uncomfortable thought aside and texted Gautam asking him to meet her immediately—she was in a desperate need of sane, sensible advice and tender loving care (not necessarily in the same order).

While Tanya was sipping coffee and commiserating with Gautam about her best friend's woeful story, her completely oblivious friend was sitting in a meeting with the said horrid guy.

The digitization project team (the content and graphics design of the Kintech team, and the Parity Global guys) had been allotted a compact workspace on the newly constructed third floor. Over the past two weeks, working in close proximity, the two teams had developed an amicable working relationship, and the weekly update meetings had lost much of its relevance as a platform to sort issues. Nitin, who had not been actively playing a part in this project, showed up at the KintechLearning office that morning. His unannounced presence was completely unexpected, even for the Parity Global team. While he had been checking with his young team on the progress on a daily basis, he had not told them about his plans to join them for the upcoming status meeting which was slated for that day.

"Hey, Nitin, you are here! Why did you not let us know that you were planning to come for the weekly meeting," exclaimed Urvashi when she spotted Nitin.

"By the way, meet Vishal Ganotra, the content development manager from KinTech. We work closely with him. Vishal, this is Nitin, our boss. Now that Nitin is here, why don't we discuss the content strategies for the next phase?"

Nitin was expecting to meet that pretty girl, Priya, and hence was a tad disappointed when he got to meet Vishal Ganotra instead. And of course, he could not ask anyone about Pirya's absence without stirring much curiosity.

Introductions over, soon it was time for the meeting to start.

"Is Priya joining, Vishal? Or should I begin," asked Anuj as he prepared to present.

"She should be joining; let me just check. Give me a minute … She is not reachable. Let us wait for five minutes, and if she doesn't show up by then, we can begin."

As they waited, Urvashi gave Nitin a quick summary of the progress made and challenges faced. Priya had not moved along with the rest of the team to the third floor as she wanted to be close to her e-learning teams. She would simply go over to meet Vishal or the Parity Global guys as and when required.

Just when Vishal was asking Anuj to begin, Priya walked in, flustered. "So sorry, guys, was stuck in another meeting. Hey, Vishal, have you started?" She was a little fazed upon seeing Nitin but recovered quickly to greet him as she took her place next to Vishal. The meeting soon commenced and Priya was cursing herself for being late and for feeling suddenly happy at seeing Nitin. She reminded herself that he was married and falling for married men was a no-no. Thankfully for her, the next agenda point caught her interest and distracted her from her chain of thoughts.

Urvashi was presenting the content strategy for the next phase of the project. Vishal had some reservations with what was being proposed by Parity Global and put forth his point of view. The discussion soon took an animated turn as diverse views were thrown across the board. Priya, sensing that the discussion was going off-track, reasoned with both parties, and proposed a workable solution that could be the way forward. With all parties agreeing to this solution, the meeting then came to a close. "Nitin, hope you are getting a hang of things in the project; I have sent you a couple of mails and meeting invites. We have a one-to-one catch-up on Thursday. Speak to you then," said Priya, politely bidding him goodbye.

Nitin spent the rest of the day with Anuj and Abhishek going over the finer details. As Nitin was leaving the building later in the evening, he saw Priya standing by the gate. She was looking at her phone and seemed to be waiting for someone. Nitin asked her if he could drop her somewhere, to which she looked surprised and told him that she was waiting for someone. At that very moment, Vishal appeared in his car and Priya left with him, turning back to wave at Nitin. As he saw her leave, smiling at something Vishal had said, he felt a twinge, almost akin to jealousy. "Soumya and Vinod are right. I need to start dating again or just get married, if this is the way I am going to react every time I see a pretty woman." He shrugged off this utterly ridiculous feeling and made plans for the evening.

# CHAPTER 8

As the weeks passed, Nitin found his resolve to be growing weaker. Every time he was at the KintechLearning office, he found himself observing Priya. He knew the reason behind such behaviour. It was only because of the endless discussions on the topic of marriage that he was staring at some woman he barely knew!

Nitin's interactions in the KintechLearning office was limited to the small Parity Global team and Vishal. He had lately been feeling bothered because of his own reaction to Vishal. For some inexplicable reason, he disliked him even though Vishal was just the kind of guy he got along with; he was smart, funny and easy to work with. Anybody working with Vishal even for a week would be able to figure out that Priya and he were good friends. His constant references to Priya during any conversation at work and their lunching or leaving together acted as constant reminders to Nitin of his silly reactions of late. What Nitin did not know was that the universe was to soon provide Nitin an opportunity to get to know Priya. On a Friday evening, the cab from KintechLearning to South Delhi met with a major accident on the highway. The two occupants present in the cab that day, both Tarun and Vishal, were thankfully alive but had suffered grave internal injuries.

With Vishal out of action for a minimum of three weeks, Priya was now to shoulder more responsibilities than before. To Nitin's pleasant surprise, he found Priya at Vishal's desk one fine morning, some three days after the unfortunate mishap that he knew nothing about till then.

"Oh, hi, Priya, you are here? Have you moved up to this floor? Where is Vishal?"

"Hello, Nitin, don't know if you heard? Vishal met with an accident last week; he will be back in a few weeks. Till then you will have to put up with me."

"Oh, I am sorry to hear that. Please convey my best wishes when you meet him next."

It had been observed by Urvashi and the boys that their boss, hitherto known to be hands-off in his approach, had changed his style of working since Priya started handling the day-to-day operations of the digitization project. Nitin had started showing up in the office almost on a daily basis. Priya accidentally overheard a related conversation one morning. As she walked to the corner where the digitization team was seated, the Parity Global team was busy discussing about the recent change in their boss's working style.

"Uru, will the boss be here today also?" asked Anuj as he chomped down a biscuit, while attempting to solve a coding puzzle.

"He is here every day these days, Anuj. Don't ask stupid questions," quipped Abhishek.

Urvashi, looking around quickly, replied, "He *is* here every day. Come to think of it, hasn't this kind of increased in the past week? He never did so for any other project. Either he has got too much free time or he is running away from home. What do you guys think?"

Abhishek chuckled, "Neither. I think it has to do with the content lead from KinTech."

"Priya?" exclaimed Urvashi, looking curious and amused.

"Oh, yes, have you not noticed that these appearances have become more frequent only after Vishal's accident?"

Urvashi frowned as she replied, "Umm, I think you have a point there, Abhishek. I think you may be right. Let us see if he shows up today. There are absolutely no meetings scheduled. And since we are the ones who do the actual work, wonder what he will do today, for there are no crises to fight, no fire to douse. Oh, here comes his call..."

The conversation was rudely interrupted by Nitin's phone call to Urvashi, giving Priya the required leeway to make an appearance. The conversation she had just heard played on a loop in her mind, disturbing whatever equilibrium she had managed to attain since Nitin entered her life. She knew not whether to be upset or excited—a strange state of affairs. While she felt somewhat flattered, it was also true that she felt completely revulsed. His showing interest (if at all this was true) suggested a morally debauched character—he was a married man with two adorable kids for heaven's sake. She had caught him staring at her, but had always attributed that to a different set of reasons. She couldn't help but wonder if she had accidentally made an ass of herself. Had she let on that she had a massive soft spot for his *model-wala avatar*, by perhaps gawking at him idiotically? Maybe that was it! Maybe, given his tendency to engage in moral debauchery, she probably was a soft target.

In short, Priya's mental mess did not get any better seeing Nitin at work that day. He had arrived a bit late than usual. The reason was his mother's arrival. She had arrived, braving the heat and dust of Delhi-NCR. Ever since Latha Ranganathan landed in Gurugram, on the pretext of staying with her grandkids and helping out her daughter—as she had no additional help, a recent development which aided her cause—she had also been occupied keeping subtle tabs on her son's whereabouts. She had been very relieved that he displayed no obvious proclivities to debauchery (be it acting or drugs or whatever else). She had been probing, subtly checking to see whether there was someone special in his life but to no avail. Latha, in a bid to get Nitin to tie the knot—if not with someone of his choice, then with someone of her choice—was in touch with long-lost relatives and friends. One never knew where the one destined for her dear son might emerge from. All this constant conversation had resulted in a whole list of prospective brides maintained meticulously by

Bharat—who had been coerced into participating—in an excel sheet, along with a folder carrying photographs tagged with the correct names.

Nitin would drop by most mornings and evenings (for a mum-made breakfast and dinner) and also to chat with her and play with his adorable nephews. This morning, seeing that he was in a generally good mood, Latha brought up the topic again while Nitin was gobbling down the dosas.

"Nitin, you had indicated you would get married, na? Do you have anyone in particular in mind?"

For a second, he was stunned. "Amma, I need to eat and go to work. *Illai yaarume illai. Naalai pesallam* (No, there is no one. Let's talk tomorrow)."

"We can talk later; but I would like you to take a look at these. Bharat, give these to him." The names, biodata and photographs were adequately produced and handed over to Nitin.

"So many? Amma, seriously, what do you want me to do? I am not even that interested. Besides I do not have the time. This Kintech project is keeping me so busy."

"See, my child, I want to see you married, and soon. Either you go through these names and come back with a shortlist, or pick one girl. You can meet them, talk to them, take your time. You know, if you know some girl you would like to marry, you can bring her to me. Anyone—she could be a north Indian, even Punjabi!"

"What?!! Nitin wants to marry a Punjabi girl? Amma, Bharat, what all have I missed?" butted in Sowmya, who up until then was speaking to a certain Major Roy Chowdhury, a constant presence in her life these days, besides Sanjay Dhamija.

Her questions were met with a stony silence and a nasty glare from Nitin. No matter how many excuses he tried to make, he was not let off. He was given a day to decide and shortlist the names, else Latha and Sowmya would do so on his behalf.

By the time he left, Nitin was rather irritated with both his mother and sister and had no clue what to do. Vinod, who called when he was on his way to KintechLearning, sensed the irritation in his voice and asked him what the matter was. Upon hearing about Nitin's plight, he gave a solid and sensible advice. There was no harm in meeting these girls or at least a couple of them. It was possible that someone might pique his interest. This set him thinking—why not Priya? He was appreciative of what he had seen of her; she was smart, professional, generally sweet and yes, he was attracted to her. Besides, now that they were working rather closely on the project, he did have an opportunity to get to know her.

Nitin entered the office, all set to strike up a friendship with Ms Priya Kaushik, who was then in the midst of a meeting that was slowly deteriorating into a mud-slinging session. With her morning getting worse by the minute, Priya was looking forward to a quiet lunch, preferably with someone she could talk to.

Anuj and Abhishek were animatedly discussing a coding issue. Seeing Nitin enter, they pulled him straight into the discussion, "Nitin, check this code, will you? We need help." The discussion and subsequent implementation of the solution went on nearly till lunchtime, which is when Priya showed up, noticeably exhausted and visibly irritated.

Nitin walked up to her, and mustering up some courage, said, "Hey, you seem stressed with work today. Would you like to join me for lunch? Would be a bit of a change."

"Oh, thanks, that's kind of you. But I am swamped with work, some other time, maybe? Sorry," Priya replied, indicating that she wished to be left alone. Much to her relief, her phone rang at the very moment. It was Vishal. "Hey Vishal, the meeting with PNGL was a disaster. Alicia kept insisting on those unreasonable deliverables. Of course, we won't be able to meet any of them."

Having been rebuffed rather subtly, one would have expected him to be nursing either a bruised ego or a broken heart. Nitin was neither conflicted nor troubled. He instead attributed her refusal to her reserved nature and work pressure, and proceeded to have lunch with his talkative team.

Priya, on the other hand, was completely torn. She barely knew how to react. She was flattered and thrilled that *he* had noticed her and wanted to have lunch with her; at the same time, she was appalled. His interest in a work colleague did not speak well about the kind of person he truly was; he must be an out and out cad. But what if he was not a cad, and maybe just stuck in a troubled marriage, she wondered. This pesky voice in her head was immediately shut down by other sensible voices. It was, after all, just a lunch invite, and that too in the office cafeteria; the man was simply being courteous and *not* expressing any other kind of interest. Grappling with all these thoughts, she heard herself refusing to lunch with him. She felt she had probably lost her last chance to be able to lunch with him at all!

Nitin's team had observed this entire exchange, with much fascination. Their rather serious boss, who never mixed his professional and personal life, had now asked a pretty colleague out for lunch. Something was going on …

# CHAPTER 9

The fascinated onlookers were in for some disappointment, as nothing substantial happened over the next few days. Nitin did show up at the KintechLearning office and was perfectly friendly with one and all, including Priya. No more lunch invites were doled out. Conversations were polite, formal, professional and fairly clipped. Such conversations would end leaving Priya irritated (with herself primarily), and leave Nitin a little bugged with himself (and also with Priya). When she refused to lunch with him, citing some excuse, he assumed that she was reserved and averse to appear being too friendly at work. However, he had been forced to revise that opinion as the project progressed. She regularly seemed to interact with people from Kintech outside work, and there were some planned lunch appointments too, and not just in the cafetaria. It probably meant it was Nitin she did not want to have lunch with.

***

The alpha version of the database for the digitization project had been released and the link sent to the librarian of one of the participating universities for user-testing. The feedback received was unfortunately worrying. Shyama Chaturvedi, the head librarian of the Seven Sisters University, which was spearheading the consortium of universities, had not only identified known and unknown bugs in the system but also indicated that the requirements had not been analysed and captured properly as desired. It was a crisis. Nitin tried to assess what could have gone wrong, between the requirement analysis and the implementation phases, while Priya tried to assuage the client to prevent any unpleasant escalations.

On a particular morning, when both Priya and Nitin were in a conference call with an impatient Shyama Chaturvedi, a tall gentleman, who otherwise was seen on the second floor, came looking for Priya.

Seeing him pass by the meeting room, Priya squealed, "I had a lunch appointment with Senthil; had completely forgotten about it. Sorry, be back in a minute."

"Never mind, you can still carry on with your lunch, if this lady ever stops her rant. However, it might become difficult for you if this call goes on for another few more hours… hmm," smiled Nitin.

Hours of trying to diffuse a crisis had left Priya with her defences down. She smiled and replied, "Ha ha, if she ever stops, I will have lunch after all and maybe with you?"

The stunned Nitin could just smile to indicate his assent.

Ms Chaturvedi's temper was finally assuaged when it was decided that Priya and Nitin would go over to Gangtok and meet her in person. She took her role as the chairperson of the consortium rather seriously. With the Seven Sisters University campus having shut for summer vacations, she was probably bored. For her, this might be a good way to keep herself occupied.

No doubt, the Parity Global team was shocked to see their boss walk into the cafeteria in Priya's company. To top it, the duo seemed so engrossed in their conversation that they did not join the others. What the team did not know was that the entire conversation was actually focused on the latest crisis in the project. The logistics around the upcoming Gangtok trip was being worked out. Other than that, Nitin attempted some small talk, but that got nowhere. Shocked by her own impulsiveness at suggesting that she lunch with Nitin, Priya was quiet and thoughtful during the lunch. She could not let this silly crush of hers get out of hand. It was decided. She would do her best to refrain from making any impulsive remark of any kind, be it in office or during the upcoming trip to Gangtok. Moreover, she felt he was being out of line by being so nice to her, for he was after all a married man. The very next moment, the rational side of her brain kicked in: *Stop it, Priya. He is a nice guy. He is talking to you and Urvashi and Sonia and everyone the way he would speak to his younger sister. Grow up!* Since Priya could not control what Nitin did or did not do, she reasoned that the least she could do was to think first and then speak—or better, not speak at all till absolutely necessary, that seeming a more doable option.

With the sudden planning of the trip to Gangtok, Vinod was now to fill up for Nitin at Kintech. The logistics involved checking Vinod's availability to travel to Delhi, and the trip was planned accordingly.

The night before Nitin was to leave, Vinod and he stopped by Sowmya's place for a quick meal. To their surprise, she was not home.

"Where is she, Amma? The house is very silent without her constant chatter," quipped Nitin, who had not spoken to his sister the past month as she had been exceptionally busy. It wasn't that sleuthing had kept Sowmya occupied. Her trusted old-time domestic help had run away! While Sowmya had been looking for clues for an extramarital affair her neighbour might be entagled in, she had missed out on what was unfolding right under her nose. Sunita, who had been with her since the time of the twins' birth, had fallen in love and eloped with a neighbour's driver. This had come to Sowmya as a jolt, for she had no clue whatsoever about the blossoming love story. Needless to say, this made her the butt of all jokes at home. Bharat, who was the only one who knew of her current sleuthing pursuits, passed cheeky remarks once in a while about her sleuthing abilities. As a result of the recent developments, Sowmya's entire focus had shifted from discovering Sharmila Batra's paramour and finding Nitin a suitable bride, to finding a new domestic help, one who was preferably single, not pregnant and, most importantly, would stay!

This hot pursuit brought her in contact with a distinct species of people. Hiring agents for domestic help came in all forms; most were outright thugs, probably involved in human-trafficking rackets, and some claimed to be poor villagers who were simply looking forward to make a quick buck. With not much experience in getting a helper, Sowmya spent most of her time contacting any and every agent whose number she could get to be able to identify a suitable candidate. As she looked far and wide (agents from as far as Noida and Indirapuram were also contacted), Sowmya got to know of a gentleman, a retired army major who had started one such agency on a purely humanitarian basis.

"My aim, to tell you frankly, Ms Sowmya, is to help people, poor people. I am a do-gooder who is concerned about the underserved people of India. I bring women from Nadia, my hometown in Bengal and rehabilitate them, get them jobs after verifying the employer," concluded the gentlemen.

Impressed with the good work he seemed to be doing, Sowmya decided that she would help in this noble endeavour and source her domestic help only through him. However, actually getting any result turned out to be a challenging experience in itself. After working with the armed forces and the bureaucratic powers that be for years, Major Roy Chowdhury was most comfortable working in a structured way. And thus, in trying to infuse some structure and professionalism in this entirely ad hoc industry, he had single-handedly devised a set of procedures. Forms detailing the specific requirements had to be filled up in triplicate and ID proofs of all family members had to be submitted well in advance. Once the prospective employers had been vetted, they were put on a waiting list. Sowmya enthusiastically filled up the forms (in triplicate), dragged Bharat and the boys for getting a perfect passport size snap clicked, got their Aadhaar cards copied and self-attested, and finally shot all these off via courier to the Major's residence in C.R. Park. Since patience was definitely not her forte, she tried expediting the process by calling the Major. However, that yielded no result and instead ended with her getting a curt reply: "Madam, I am analysing your requirements and looking for a perfect match." Finally, after a week, a suitable potential match was found. Sowmya was expected to be present at quarter past six the next evening to meet the prospective bride … oops the domestic help, and be interviewed. It was easy getting mixed up with her pursuits, with one taking precedence over the other in her head at times. From Gurugram, Sowmya went all the way to little Kolkata, that too in peak rush hours. To her surprise, she wasn't able to meet the domestic help that easily. The old Major, a rather eccentric Bengali gentleman, interrogated and scrutinized her with a barrage of questions: Was she who she claimed she was? Did they have any perverse habits back home? Would they treat the domestic help well?

Once he was convinced that this slightly scatter-brained, fidgety woman in front of him was who she said she was, the potential domestic help was presented. Sowmya was then given the opportunity to interview her and vice versa. The interview process, once successful and complete, Sowmya picked up the maid, luggage and all, and left for Gurugram.

Sowmya and the newly hired domestic help made an appearance midway through the dinner at her house. "Hey, Vinod, you are back! And Nitin, how are you, my dear?" screeched Sowmya as she ruffled Nitin's hair.

"Why don't you join us for dinner, Sowmya?" suggested Vinod.

"She will, she will, once she has figured out what's going on and instructed everyone," quipped Bharat.

"Indeed! Give me ten minutes."

Sowmya did just that. Taking a quick update from her mother as to what had gone on at home during her three-hour absence, she then went about completing her remaining chores for the day, like getting the kids ready for bed, putting them to sleep, so on and so forth. Once she was done with that, she spent some time instructing the new help, showing her around the house. Meanwhile, the animated conversation at the dinner table, which had previously covered topics from Trump to Hemanta Biswas, from Federer to Kohli, had veered towards the KintechLearning project when Sowmya joined them to eat. As she sat listening to Nitin and Vinod discussing the challenges in the project, Sowmya remembered the "pretty Priya" reference from one of their previous conversations. Instead of ribbing her brother, she instead addressed Vinod, "Aha, so you will be spending a week at the KintechLearning office? Do convey my regards to pretty Priya."

"No such luck, Sowmya. Pretty Priya is travelling to Gangtok with our dear Nitin," guffawed Vinod.

This bit of information triggered the interest of both Sowmya and Latha, who was sitting on the couch switching TV channels.

"Achcha Nitin, have you got to know this girl? Is she still as pretty as you found her back then?"

"And where is she from? What exactly does she do?"

The questions came in quick succession from both the women, much to Nitin's horror. Luckily for him, Bharat stepped in to his rescue. "Let him be. Poor guy. It is just some work colleague, Sowmya. Just because she is pretty doesn't mean shit."

Even as Nitin was thanking his brother-in-law for stepping in, he thought how wrong Bharat was. Priya may just be a work colleague, but she was very pretty and he did have the hots for her. He was looking forward to this two-day trip to Gangtok.

At the same time, in the small flat in GK, Tanya was helping Priya pack. She seemed more enthusiastic than Priya. "Gangtok will be lovely at this time of the year. Arre, you are getting to go for a couple of days away from the dusty, dirty, hot Delhi. Baba, Priya, please do not look so sad. Who is this work colleague who is accompanying you? Are you sad because of the person?"

"It's not that I am sad. I just don't want to go. This trip is totally unnecessary. That Ms Chaturvedi is one crazy woman—she initially shared a different set of requirements, and now she wants something else. She is happily blaming us—both KintechLearning and Parity Global. Imagine, she is now refuting the approved, finalized documentation. For us, at Kintech, the client is bhagwaan, and hence we are at her service. I am going with Nitin … he heads Parity Global."

"You do not bother about that mad lady. Enjoy the nice cab ride from Bagdogra. The scenery is awesome. Ever since you told me about your trip, I have been trying to convince Gautam to go on a holiday—a nice long romantic one. Ha, ha, think of it, you may even spot your paan masala dude in other ads," chuckled Tanya, leading to Priya throwing a pillow at her head.

"My paan masala dude, indeed!"

This conversation of course increased her apprehension about the entire trip and her general state of nervousness. She barely slept that night.

# CHAPTER 10

When Nitin met Priya at the boarding gate in the airport the next day, he observed that she seemed preoccupied . She also came across as more aloof.

"All okay? You look a bit stressed," Nitin checked on her once they had finished boarding.

"Hmm, it's just that I am a nervous flier," replied Priya looking somewhat dazed.

"You can hold my hand if you want to," offered Nitin, with a charming smile.

Not knowing how to respond and in order to avoid gawking, Priya smiled and took out a book to read. She clearly was not interested in having a long conversation with him, or so it seemed to him. But Nitin was not one to be dissuaded so easily. He had made up his mind to get to know this sweet, funny girl he was sitting next to.

"What are you reading?"

Realizing that she couldn't sit gaping at the book or him, and that ignoring him through the entire flight was also not possible, Priya merely mumbled a response hoping he would end the conversation himself, finding her to be the most boring person on earth. But that did not happen. Instead, she found herself being questioned about inane things and was forced to contribute to the conversation.

"Aargh! Is this what passes off as upma these days?" cribbed Nitin as he looked at the upma in the ready-to-make packet in front of him.

"You like upma? Who likes upma?"

"Umm, you don't?"

"Not what you get in this airline, certainly not. I like the upma my mother makes."

"Which means you haven't had the upma you get in CTR … Aren't you from the city?" asked Nitin, trying to confirm what he knew because it seemed that she had never heard of CTR before.

"Appa and Amma live there, so perhaps I am. What about you? Out and out from there?"

"Oh yes, out and out Bengaluru guy—NPS, RVCE and then IIM. Sample the upma from CTR before you make up your mind."

"CTR Malleshwaram? Isn't that the place for benne dosas? Or is that Vidyarthi Bhavan? Well, never mind." Even before Priya realized it, she had been drawn into a conversation that uncovered certain common topics of interest, many similarities in personality and circumstances. They seemed to be developing a rapport and comfort level. By the time they reached the vast campus of Seven Sisters University, Priya and Nitin were now slightly less than the strangers they had been before.

The meeting with Ms Chaturvedi was quite eventful. Playing the part of a dissatisfied client came rather naturally to the librarian and she made it known, much to Priya's displeasure, who found her behaviour to be entirely unprofessional and unacceptable. The requirements had been negotiated, agreed upon and documented, so how could this lady suddenly do a volte-face? With a fair sense of right and wrong, and being a confident, assertive person, Priya was on the verge of stating her point loud and clear. She was also close to coming across as a strident activist—definitely not the approach required for this meeting. Before things could go completely downward, Nitin stepped in, deftly tackling the annoyed Ms Chaturvedi, with all his charm.

While the tactic definitely worked on the intended target, it also worked in leaps and bounds on Priya. She sat, observing, actually staring at him, wordlessly, charmed and utterly resigned. It was a moment that was going to be imprinted in her memory. As the realization sunk in, the poor girl was in a complete whirlpool of emotions—smitten, tongue-tied and terribly tormented. Her rational mind was waging a lone battle as she felt herself sink into this whirlpool. Thankfully, before she could make a complete ass of herself, for she sat gawking like a lovestruck duck, her phone started pinging—not once, not twice, but thirty-five times in quick succession. This prompted Nitin to turn towards her and caustically whisper, "You should tell your boyfriend to not disturb you. You are in a meeting, a serious one at that. Oh wait, does he even work?"

The comment definitely worked as an antidote. Priya was back in her usual element. "Whoever it is, who is trying to get through to me, knows that I am in a meeting. There are more important things in life than just work. Of course, you probably wouldn't know," Priya whispered back to him, with irritation evident in her response. Glaring at him, she switched off the phone. She was also feeling frustrated with whomsoever it was who had been pinging her back to back. Finally, the meeting came to an end, a successful one at that. The deft handling had worked wonders. Ms Chaturvedi was charmed and suitably pacified by now. Once her ego had been assuaged, she was okay proceeding with what had been earlier approved. So once the bugs in the system were fixed, the alpha version was good to go.

As Nitin and Priya walked out of Ms Chaturvedi's room in silence, Priya switched on her phone. Fifty-five message notifications and three missed call alerts popped up.

"Think it is time that you call your boyfriend and put an end to his misery," sniggered Nitin, startling Priya out of her reverie and prompting her to drop the phone. "Oh, shoot!" Nitin got to the phone quicker than Priya did. It was sheer curiosity and part jealousy that prompted him to be extra chivalrous. Throughout the meeting, he kept wondering who it was and, most importantly, why was that person so desperate and eager to speak to Priya. It was obvious that it was not anything serious, else she would have answered the text messages right away instead of switching off the phone. The slipping phone from her hand provided him with a golden opportunity to catch it and check its screen. And he did—only to wish he did not. Nitin was not happy to note that both last missed call and message were from Vishal Ganotra. "So, you are dating Vishal! He isn't bad, though you could do better," teased Nitin as he handed over her phone.

Poor Priya, already embarrassed at her clumsiness, was now absolutely stunned at Nitin's assumption that Vishal Ganotra was her boyfriend. Since she knew that she would only blabber, given the tongue-tied lovestruck idiot that she was, she did not bother dismissing the assumption. She took the phone back, thanked him, and added, "He *does* work, by the way."

As they walked towards the executive guest house, where they were put up for the day, in a moment of total irrationality, Priya called Vishal, in front of Nitin, and sounded extremely sweet. Vishal, not used to being so much sweetness directed at him, was shocked.

"Are you alright, Priya?

"Gangtok is so beautiful. We must come here soon. Together."

"What??! What is wrong with you? What nonsense are you blabbing?"

"Bye, you take care, dear. I need to go. That Parity Global guy is waiting here," quipped Priya, knowing fully well that Nitin would have heard some part of the conversation.

As soon as she cut the call, her rational mind once again took over. *Idiot, now what if Vishal thinks you are flirting with him? Do you think this married man cares whether Vishal or that tea-stall-wala there is your boyfriend?*

The cold truth of her stupid impulsive action exacerbated her already foul mood. She tried to shake herself out of her despondency by now reading the remaining fifty-four messages. It was Tanya who had been going berserk trying to reach her.

> *Pri.*
>
> *Call me back!*
>
> *Matter of life and death!*
>
> *It is of prime importance, else your friend shall die!*
>
> *Pri, why are you not answering my messages? You aren't even picking my call!*
>
> *Priya Kaushik, you have been in Gangtok for a day and you have forgotten me already. You don't pick up my calls any more!*
>
> *Ok, here it goes. Salman Khan is in Gangtok this evening. I so need an autograph. Print my pic and get it signed. Can you do that much for me? Please please please ... You know I love Salman!*

And the messages went on, in a similar vein and tone. Priya was exasperated. "She is totally jobless."

"Who is jobless? Your boyfriend who keeps messaging you?" Nitin butted in. Curiosity and jealousy seemed to have taken over his usual restraint.

"Arre, no, not my boyfriend," said Priya, rolling her eyes.

Nitin thought it was a completely normal and spontaneous gesture, but it left him a little breathless, much to his own surprise. He struggled a bit to ask, "Then who?"

Priya looked at him vaguely, wondering what was wrong with him. *Is Nitin actually conversing with me? Is it me or does he look a little dazed, a little lost? It is me. He probably knows I am a besotted fool? Shit. What should I do? Be normal, girl. Reply. Talk. It would be better than gaping like a fish.*

"It was my crazy flatmate, Tanya. And, she is this *huge* Salman Khan fan. Salman Khan is apparently here in Gangtok shooting for some movie. I am now supposed to locate him, wherever he is, and then get his autograph for her. She is nuts. She always does something like this. There was this time when we were in college ..."

Seeing Priya go on about her flatmate, with exasperation and affection in equal halves, something struck a chord within Nitin. He felt protective of the utterly charming young lady in front of him, almost wanting to pull her into his arms right then. Better sense and years of restraint prevailed as he sought to understand his own involuntary reactions. A thirty-year-old man is hardly likely to fall in love just like that, becoming utterly besotted.

"Sorry, I have gone on and on and bored you to death," said Priya, stopping after a long tirade, when she realized Nitin had gone quiet.

"Nothing like that. Really. I was a bit preoccupied."

"Bored, you mean," smiled Priya, good-naturedly as Nitin looked rather shamefaced.

Before he could say anything, his phone rang; a crisis had cropped up in another project and required his immediate attention. With Nitin hurrying back to his room in the executive guest house, Priya decided to walk around the campus to clear her head and get a grip on things. The poor girl realized she was in a precarious position—even her crushes during school and college days hadn't been this idiotic. There had been a flurry of those, but nothing lasting beyond a couple of days other than that heartbreaking relationship with Karthik. However, that was ages ago. Priya was certain that she was no longer carrying any remnant of that heartbreak. She was sure she was okay—or was she not, she suddenty wondered? After all, how could a supposedly sane and sensible young woman become infatuated with a married man.

Was it because it had been too long since she had dated someone? *Blast that Karthik, damn him. Maybe I should ask Vishal out for a date. Eww, no. Why Vishal? Stop it, Priya. You are becoming like Tanya ... or maybe I could agree to meet one of those guys, Amma and Appa keep coming up with. I need to go back home.* Wistful and almost homesick, as she walked, directionless, literally and metaphorically, she came across a building that looked like a common area for students of both the technical and medical faculties.

A large colourful poster posted by the university's retro film fan club announcing the weekly screening caught Priya's attention. If there was one thing that would take her attention from her self-created, imagined problem, it was this. Priya was a major movie buff; any language, any genre, black-and-white,

Eastmancolor, technicolour—anything would do. There was one small condition. The movie had to be made before 1980! Of course, she had her preferences and within this vast selection too. The movie being screened later by the film club that evening starred a particular favourite. Long before she lusted after a certain model in a shady ad, she had lusted rather badly for a certain Hindi movie star. Maybe it was his smile, the way he moved on the screen, the type of roles he did, and the innate charm and sex appeal he had. Whatever it was, Priya was smitten. He was a serious obsession, and all of that would have been fine but for the fact that, just as in the case of her current object of interest, the star in question was married and had two kids. Thankfully, the similarities ended at that. In fact, the movie star in question, unlike the current object of interest, was old enough to be her grandfather. Shammi Kapoor had graduated to playing grandfather roles in movies by the time Priya Kaushik was born.

And, undoubtedly, it was a Shammi Kapoor poster that had attracted her attention. Regardless of the fact that she had probably seen the movie some 101 times, she walked up to the building and made quick enquiries. She was soon face-to-face with her first true love, albeit separated by a large screen. Nitin was forgotten for the time being.

Meanwhile, Nitin, after having solved pressing issues that could have had a detrimental effect on his livelihood, decided to go on a long trek. Unlike Priya, who had forgotten about her colleague for a while, he had not. He seemed to be thinking more and more about her. Her eyes, dreamy and fish-like;

her lopsided smile and the way it lit up the entire room; and her voice, low and husky, seeming to fill his mind with sheer joy. The initial attraction seemed to be slowly building into a case of serious lust. And worse, he wanted to spend more time with her, not necessarily in bed (*which would be good too,* he thought) but simply even sitting and watching her would have also sufficed, getting to observe her when she rolled her eyes in exasperation, her vivid face, bright and glowing, lit up with fleeting expressions of a myriad kind.

As he set out for the trek around the campus in the mountains, just before sunset, such dreamy thoughts seemed to fill his mind, making him wonder with awe and surprise—could she be the one who completes the other half of his heart? Thankfully, being of a practical disposition now at the age of thirty and not degenerating to his younger emotional self, he decided to go look for her and check what her plans for dinner were. It was after all always good to get to know the person who was so dominating one's thoughts. The only hitch was that her phone was switched off. Blaming the poor network in the mountains, he decided to go and check up on her in person. She was not in her room either, much to his disappointment. Where had she gone?

Since dinner was pending, and Priya was just not reachable, Nitin decided to go try a nearby joint which was said to have the best momo in the area. To his astonishment, he saw Priya seated there, in the company of two north-eastern students, laughing heartily. He was now no longer astonished but somewhat piqued. Could she have not checked with him if she had decided to go ahead for dinner? And who were these kids?

Basking in cinematic heaven in a small room, oohing and aahing as Shammi Kapoor performed his antics on screen, along with just two other seemingly mad movie buffs, Priya had had a blast that evening. Tsen Dorje and Angel Omato, the two others at the screening, were the main student officials of the not-so-popular movie club. Truth be told, they were thrilled when Priya had come up to enquire about the screening. For Tsen and Angel, childhood sweethearts and natives of Gangtok, old Hindi films screened regularly in small shacks passing off as theatres had been a major source of entertainment and solace while growing up. It had become a lifelong obsession. It was disappointing for them that not many of their fellow students at the campus appreciated these films. While popular movie screenings were a big hit, the retro ones were hardly attended. The duo, who also officiated another movie club, were not to be deterred, and thus old movies were screened regularly in a bid to generate interest among the locals. Alas, since not many viewers had shown up or expressed interest, they had been on the verge of cancelling the screening just before Priya had walked up to them. By intermission, Priya had become friends with the two and made dinner plans with them for the night. She did think of Nitin at that moment. She would have informed him but her phone was discharged by then and she had also forgotten the power bank back in her room. That was how Priya, with a wee bit of guilt, had landed up at the momo place with Tsen and Angel.

As Nitin was about to be seated, of course at a different table, Priya turned around and spotted him. "Nitin, come and join us," said Priya, genuinely happy to see him. Such an enthusiastic welcome was bound to warm the cockles of Nitin's heart. And just like that, with a smile, Priya had captivated Nitin. Seated next to her, as introductions were made, he heard everything that had happened since afternoon. Of course, she did not let out the bit about Shammi Kapoor. It sufficed to say that she was an old Hindi movie buff. Did Nitin watch movies? Yes, he did but with no such passion or reverence. A lively conversation about movies ensued, as three of the four people at the table seemed to be devout cinephiles. Nitin watched, fascinated, as Priya went about having a lively animated discussion on various aspects of the silver screen. She sure loved movies! Other topics also did come up, as the students were keen to know more about their guests. Did the two work in the same office? What did they do? Where were they from? What did they like doing? Were they coming to Gangtok for the first time? Once the barrage of questions were answered, anecdotes shared, the two walked towards their respective rooms. It almost seemed to the two that now they had a bond, almost akin to friendship.

# CHAPTER 11

The return journey was fairly uneventful, with time passing by in a relaxed companionable silence. When they landed in Delhi airport, it was rather late in the night.

"How are you going back? Should I drop you home?" asked an attentive Nitin.

"No, no, thanks, not needed. Tanya, I told you about her, and her boyfriend Gautam will be here."

"Ah, the girl who wanted Salman Khan's autograph!"

"Shoot, I completely forgot about Salman Khan. Tanya will give me hell," cried Priya in absolute horror.

"Ha, ha, you should tell her that Shammi Kapoor trumps Salman Khan, any day."

"True that. Can't tell her, though. I shall never be forgiven. The amount of emotional blackmail, I would be subject to, is unimaginable."

"Don't worry, I will help you cook up some story if need be," smiled Nitin as they waited outside the airport. Priya looked around, trying to come up with a believable story in her head, while Nitin looked at his phone.

"Priiiiiii, you are back! Did you get it? Did you get to see him?!" squealed an excited Tanya as she spotted Priya from a distance and ran towards her.

Amused, Nitin looked at her and asked: "All set to lie through your teeth?" Priya, extremely embarrassed at this show on her dear friend's part, nodded smilingly.

"Is this affection for *you*? Or for the fact that you may have met Salman and have his autograph with you?"

"Partly both is what I would think," said Priya, as she found herself being completely engulfed in a bear hug.

As soon as she was released, Priya introduced Tanya to Nitin, "Tanya, meet my colleague, Nitin."

"Good to meet you, Nitin," replied Tanya, extending a hand forward, staring at him. "Actually, you seem familiar. Have we met before?"

Nitin looked surprised, "Not sure. Sorry, if we have, I don't seem to remember."

Pleasantries exchanged, they went their separate ways. As soon as Priya got into the car, to her relief, Tanya seemed to have forgotten about Salman Khan. But the next moment, she was subjected to a strict interrogation.

"Prii, now spit. *What are you doing with the paan masala dude???* You said you were going to Gangtok with a work colleague. *This is your work colleague??* Do you even know what you are doing? Good Lord, here I get busy with my own saga, and you go and start dating a paan masala ad model!"

"Shut up, Tanya. He is who I said he was. Nitin Ranganathan, he heads Parity Global. It was a bloody work trip. Stop hyperventilating. And, I am not dating him. Chill."

Tanya calmed down but was looking rather perturbed. "You never told me you had met him in real life. We do need to talk, in detail, once we get back home."

Needless to say, the discussion at home lasted half the night. Priya told her friend everything, right from the time she met him briefly at the airport to the just concluded Gangtok trip. "He is a married man with two kids, Tanya. Will you now please stop worrying about my so-called futile infatuation!"

"Oh, you already know he is married? I was wondering how to break it to you. I have met his wife," said Tanya quietly.

"You have met his wife? Where? How?"

"Has he been flirting with you, Priya?"

"Huh, no. He is a nice guy, a work colleague, that is all."

"Attentive to you?"

"What are you getting at?"

"Nothing, absolutely nothing. Please remember there are better guys out there. You just focus on work. Do nothing! Just don't do anything you shouldn't do."

"Tanya, I know you are worried about me, but I am not an idiot. Don't worry."

"How can I not? I was there when that Karthik dumped you for that firang girl. Horrible man. You shall not, I repeat, you shall not speak with him."

"I do not speak with Karthik. Why should I? I don't even know where he is. Maybe Melbourne or was it Sydney—what does it matter?"

"I meant, don't speak with this Nitin paan masala chap. *Koi daana mat daalo*. All these men are haraamis, I tell you. As soon as they spot a pretty girl, they start taking advantage. And this one is definitely not to be trusted. Arre, his own wife doesn't trust him. Let me tell you where I met her. At a detective's office. Imagine."

"A detective's office? Huh? What were you there for?"

"Uh, oh, you see Pri, I was hopeful that Dhamija-ji would be able to trace this paan masala guy for you ..."

"What?!! You went there to look for this paan masala guy—because you thought I am in love with him?"

"You were keeping his pic and sleeping."

"What! When?"

"I found the *Grihshobha* next to your pillow."

"Nonsense, if you had bothered reading that magazine, you would have seen that there was a write-up on Shammi Kapoor. And just because I ogle at an ad does not mean shit. God! Tanya, you are too much. By the way, what does his wife do?"

"Oh, his wife is the detective's partner. Isn't that cool? She too solves cases. Maybe I should also offer to help out."

Priya did not know what to say. Tanya was getting crazier by the day. God help them all.

"How does one become a detective, Priya?"

"How would I know? This sounds shady, Tanu. Now, this lady, what's her name? Why don't you ask her?"

"Haan, I could. But what do you have to do with her name anyway… Having so much curiosity is not healthy. Did the guy not tell you his wife's name?"

Priya was quiet. Come to think of it, Nitin never spoke about his wife or his kids. Strange.

"Nahin, he never speaks about them."

"Haww, Priya, please stay away from that man. He seems to be a horrible person. Do not talk to him, or even smile at him. Don't add to it in any way, okay?

"Okay, okay, baba, now let me sleep," said Priya, tired of being lectured. God knows what new drama awaited her at work the next day.

The next day did usher in more drama but not of the kind Priya had anticipated. Work was more or less the way it had been. Crises had to be dealt with, meetings attended, emails responded to, all within the time frame of eight hours. Upon reaching office, Priya also found out from the Parity Global guys that their boss had been called away to Mumbai for another project. That Nitin was to be away for a couple of weeks provided Priya much relief. Time enough to regain what little sense she thought she had.

The next couple of weeks passed by quicker than anticipated. When Nitin returned, he was in for a surprise. Vishal was back in his cubicle and Priya was nowhere to be seen at their cosy corner. After some not-so-discreet inquiries from Urvashi and the boys, he found out that Priya had shifted back to her second-floor cabin and had actually not been seen much the past week. This continued for the next seven days too. Nitin and Priya hardly got to meet each other.

Concentrating full-time on the two e-learning accounts Priya handled meant that her workload had considerably increased. In a bid to keep her mind clear of any unwanted, distracting thoughts, she had also started participating in quizzing. She had been a part of the quizzing circuit earlier but dropped off the radar after she got progressively busy. She found an easy entry back to the circuit, thanks to Gautam, an active and founding member of the Dillikwizzers; he also spent all his weekends participating in the numerous quizzes organized in the Delhi-NCR circuit. Dillikwizzers, now in existence for over half a decade, was the brainchild of two JNU PhD students, who had teamed up with three other friends, including Gautam and his then roommate Abhishek Pillai. Within five years, quizzing had regained its losing popularity, with IIT lecture halls becoming the venue, and people across the spectrum, such as corporate professionals, engineers, civil servants and scholars, participating in these regularly held events. Every February, the founders hosted the biggest quizzing competition in Delhi.

Since the time Priya had found out about the quizzing events Gautam organized, she had been making plans to join him. These plans finally materialized and she had spent the last two weekends teaming up with Gautam for these quizzes. The coming Sunday was supposed to be a biggie. Abhishek and his wife Ramya were even planning to come down to Delhi to attend the big event. Gautam and Priya were planning to team up with Abhishek for both the written round and then, if they qualified, for the final round. Tanya too had agreed to go with them, not because she liked or enjoyed quizzing, but because she was fond of Abhishek and Ramya. Come Friday evening, the plans fizzled out when Abhishek called and said that he and his wife wouldn't be able to make it. Gautam and Priya were left with one missing partner for the next day's quiz. Last-minute calls were being made by both as they tried checking among friends and acquaintances to see whether anyone would be interested in joining them as the third team member for the next day's quiz. With no names coming up, Priya decided to arm-twist Vishal into joining her. With this in mind, she went up to the Parity Global corner where Nitin, who had made a belated appearance that day, was busy brainstorming a potential solution with Vishal.

"Long time, no see. All good?" beamed Nitin, really happy to see her again after two weeks. He wouldn't have admitted it—neither to himself nor to anyone else—but he had kind of missed her.

"Yes, yes long time. How are you? Ah, I see, I am interrupting you guys. But Vishal, call me back when free."

"Not really, we are almost done. Vishal is all yours," quipped Nitin, happiness immediately replaced by a childish jealousy. He was also about to vacate the seat and move to his own cabin.

"Oh, no, please, you can stay. Vishal, what are you doing tomorrow?"

"Dragging myself all the way to Pitampura to attend some distant cousin's engagement. Why?"

"You aren't free then?

"No, but what happened?"

"Remember I told you about the quiz tomorrow?"

"The one which Gautam and you were attending with some friend of his? At IIT?"

"Yeah, but now Abhishek cannot come and we are in desperate need of a third person so that we can participate."

"Why don't you drag Tanya?"

"Her being there or not is just the same. She is our absolute last-ditch go-to person."

Nitin, who had been overhearing this conversation with much interest, said, "You quiz?"

Priya looked up, surprised at this rather obvious question, and nodded.

"Cool, count me in. I will join you and your friend. Message me the details."

"You quiz??"

Nitin beamed, "Used to, back in Bengaluru. Hardly have time now. Didn't know there was an active quizzing scene around here."

Surprised to find a shared common interest and relieved to have found a third partner, Priya smiled, saying she would send him all the required details. She then hurried away to convey the good news to Gautam.

When Tanya heard from Gautam that Nitin was to team up with them for the next day's quiz, she was genuinely worried. She brought up the topic with Priya, as she joined Tanya and Gautam for their Friday-night dinner.

"Why did you call him, Priya? Were you not able to find anybody else?"

Priya, not happy at being chastised, protested. "I did not call him, Tanya. Stop imagining things!"

"He *was* a quizzer? Really? His intentions seem to be rather doubtful to me."

Before it could escalate into an argument, Gautam stepped in, "It's just a quiz, baby. Besides, I will be there with Priya. And besides, thanks to him, Priya and I can attend the event now. And maybe this Nitin is a genuine quizzer, as he claims to be."

As Priya kept mum, preferring to focus on the food in front of her, Tanya decided that she would attend the quiz too. She had to be there, to keep an eye on her dearest friend. She had a better sense of discernment when it came to men and their intentions, compared to her spaced-out friend, and hence she should be there to suss out that man and his intentions. Gautam and Priya smiled, listening to Tanya's passionate monologue. They were simply happy to know that their quiz plans had not been jeopardized.

The quiz turned out to be a success. Nitin, despite Tanya's misgivings, was indeed an avid quizzer, competitive and well informed. With varied interests, the team actually complemented each other, playing off their strengths and weaknesses. They aced the written round, and stood second in the final round in which they competed against nine teams. As the event came to an end, shortly around early evening, plans were made to go out for a dinner at the nearby SDA market.

Contrary to Tanya's expectations, Nitin tried to excuse himself, but Gautam wouldn't hear of it. So, the four of them landed up at the upscale pizzeria, dissecting the happenings of the day and making plans for the quiz the next weekend. It almost was as if Nitin had become a part of the team, much to Tanya's apparent displeasure.

The following Monday, When they met outside the elevator at work, Nitin asked Priya, "The lecture hall in IIT, is it the venue for all quizzes?"

"Most of the time. Though the one, this coming Saturday, is likely to be in faraway Noida, at the Amity campus. Gautam said he would confirm by Thursday."

"Aargh, Noida is far. Not sure if I would like to drive down all that distance."

"Yep, it is extremely far from Gurugram."

"Maybe you can stay over at some friend's place on Friday?"

"Hmm, perhaps. Talking of friend, your friend Tanya doesn't seem to like me much, does she?" smiled Nitin.

Priya uncomfortably said, "No, no, not that. She wasn't at her friendliest on Saturday. She gets bored in quizzes."

"Ha, ha, I got the impression that I was under some intense scrutiny. She was shooting daggers at me through the dinner."

Thankfully, by now Priya reached her floor and managed to scoot, making a mental note to chastise Tanya for her behaviour that day. Nitin, clearly, was no fool. While it was true that he was an avid quizzer, he had not been free that Saturday. There was an important prior engagement with his mother that he had had to cancel, just to be able to attend the quiz—not that he had forgotten about the engagement while confirming to Priya of his availability. The truth was he had been pleasantly surprised at finding out that Priya too quizzed. This was also an opportunity to spend more time with her without being too obvious. The flipside was that he had had to lie to his mother after years, citing office work as the reason for this late cancellation! Obviously, having had to do this at thirty was irking him and he *felt* like a fool. And then there was this whole bit of Tanya shooting murderous glances throughout the dinner. Was he that obvious in showing his interest? Or did she disapprove of him, preferring Vishal instead for her friend. *Vishal was rather conventionally good-looking,* he ruefully thought.

# CHAPTER 12

In the coming weeks, Tanya continued to tail Priya and Gautam for each and every quizzing event. Nitin also became a regular; regardless of whether the event would be held in Delhi or Noida, he'd cancel family engagements with a straight face if need be. He was a competitive guy, and these quizzes fuelled his competitiveness further. Spending time with Priya then became an added bonus. It was becoming more and more evident to Tanya that a bond was developing between her dear friend and this "married" guy who had wormed his way into the group. It was rather obvious, and she explained it to Gautam one Sunday evening as the team was walking into a café in the local SDA market post quiz. "Oh Gautam, just look at them. Those smiles, the stolen glances. Just see how he keeps looking at her. And she is smiling. Uff, Gautam, what do I do! *Meri sabse achchi friend, jise main sensible samajhti thhi, gadhi nikli.*" Gautam, who till then had been slightly dismissive of Tanya and her paranoid worries about Nitin's intentions, found himself observing them and agreeing with Tanya.

Something had started brewing between Priya and Nitin—whether or not they admitted to it, to themselves or others.

"What to do?" asked Tanya

"What can we do, baby?" replied Gautam.

"Speak to Priya maybe? Make her see sense? This definitely doesn't look like it's going in the right direction. Or why don't you change your quiz partner?"

"How would that help? He will find other opportunities to meet Priya, who looks all too willing herself!"

"Point, atleast we are here to see what this man is up to. Priya is an idiot!" said Tanya, finding herself cosily enveloped in Gautam's warm hug.

Shortly after this discussion, which of course ended abruptly, Tanya, not known to keep things lying down for a while, decided to confront it head-on.

A few days later, manoeuvring a conversation with Nitin alone, she asked him point-blank about his interest in Priya.

Nitin, who had not realized till then that his interest in Priya had become both serious and obvious, recoiled at the question and nodded in reply. "I like her. Why?"

Tanya, who had been equally shocked at her question and his candid reply, said, "Nitin, how can you so shamelessly admit your feelings for Priya? Really, this is too much. Such a cad, rake and, what was that word, profli— something?"

"Profligate," prompted Nitin, irritated.

"Profligate, thank you!"

As Tanya stormed away after exhausting her newly acquired vocabulary, poor Nitin was left wondering exactly what bit of his answer rendered him shameless. Liking someone and admitting that is objectionable? Profligate? Rake? That girl was deranged. Crazy, immature girl! What a contrast to Priya! How are these two even friends?

In the larger scheme of things, this taking-the-bull-by-its-horns approach by Tanya was to prove rather cataclysmic. Nitin spent that Sunday evening and part of the night reflecting upon Tanya's words. The more he thought about it, he was surer about what he wanted and what he had to do. Priya had started occupying a large chunk of space in his heart and mind. What began as a physical reaction to her attractive self, he was now besotted by her pretty eyes, long, straight, silky hair and that vibrant, lopsided smile. This magnetic attraction had blossomed into a fondness, an affection beyond description. He wanted to be near her, with her for as long as he could be. A mix of desire, attraction, fondness and affection—if this is not love, what is? By the time dawn broke, ushering in another day, his mind was made up. Quite the romantic that he was, he would now declare his intentions. Priya would be wooed and how! If Tanya thought this was shamelessness on his part in pursuit of her dear friend, she should watch out now.

As it often happens, some plans get rather delayed on the execution front. Poor Nitin, in his romantic and poetic ardour, was soon to realize that his "woo the girl" plan would have to be deferred to a much later date.

While Nitin was introspecting and envisaging a future with Priya, their big house, two kids, dog and all, Priya was being schooled by Tanya and how!

"You are an idiot. Have you lost your mind?"

"What have I done now?"

"No, no, bat your eyelids, coyly smile some more, saying 'That's so funny, Nitin,'" mocked Tanya.

"I do not do that. Stop it, Tanya."

"You are in love, Priya Kaushik, with a bloody married man. And you are telling me to shut up."

"Look, I like him, very much, yes… What can I even do about it…"

"Nitin is a jerk—he as much admitted to me that he liked you."

"He did?"

"Don't look pleased, idiot."

"Tanu, why does this happen to me always? First Karthik, and now Nitin."

"Priya, my once-upon-a-time-sensible friend, please *sudhar jao*. Remember, he is a married man, has two kids, probably has a third coming on the way."

"I do not wish to know…"

"The point is you have to get a grip on this. He is a shameless man. Remember, I told you that his wife is an associate of that detective Dhamija."

"Yeah."

"Do you know how she became his associate? She met him first as his client. She hired him to track Nitin's movements.

Can you not see what kind of a person he is. Please stay away from him!"

Feeling rather quashed at getting to know that Nitin may not be so innocent after all and that his wife was suspecting him of infidelity, Priya threw herself on the bed, melodramatically, "Okay, you do have a point… I am getting carried away. I have been spending so much time with him, at work, lunch, quizzes. But Tanu, he does seem so nice, attentive, caring ... Uff! Anyway, I promise to behave."

Even though the conversation was formally over, neither of the girls could sleep that night. Priya was feeling rather despondent; she knew not why. She now had proof that he was a cad and hence should not be obsessed over. But … he liked her, and she liked him too. What a complete mess. Tragic, to be precise. She had a penchant for falling for people who either did not reciprocate her feelings or were already taken. Maybe, it was time she got an appointment with a shrink? Or maybe it was time to simply go home—it had been a while. Tanya, on the other hand, was worried about her friend and was thinking of ways to help her.

By dawn, both of them had resolved to act upon the situation. Priya decided to pay heed to Tanya's advice and limit all conversations and interactions with Nitin to a purely professional level. Meanwhile, Tanya decided to go and meet Dhamija. Sowmya deserved to know that her husband was such a cad and openly showing interest in other women! For the sake of helping her fellow sisters, the truth must be told. Dhamija would be the right person to break this to Sowmya.

In his years of being a detective, Sanjay Dhamija had figured out that the summer months of May and June are the worst. His business, almost always, saw a dip in these months. There just weren't that many cases to occupy his times in these months. The whys and wherefores of this was debated heatedly at home often. Anita, his beloved wife, put it down to the lethargy caused by this relentless heat, "Arre, who will leave their house in this heat, and if people do not leave their house, how will they indulge in affairs or murders? And if they don't, obviously you will not find much work."

Dhamija blamed it on the vacations: "The entire family packs up and leaves for a vacation somewhere or the other. So when the wife is constantly hovering around, what would the poor husband do?"

Naturally, the husband and wife were not happy about this slowdown in business. For Anita, this had added repercussions, for Dhamija spent more time at home, which was an intrusion definitely not appreciated by Anita.

"He keeps giving me a headache the entire time," Anita confided in Sanvi. "You please take him to office somehow, even if there is no work. In fact, let us set up a TV for him. Doing so, he can kill the time he wants sitting in front of the TV."

While Anita was plotting ways to get her husband out of their house, one summer morning, a few weeks later, Tanya called Dhamija, requesting for his time for an urgent matter. She had to meet him that very day. The office was opened up and the dolts Hari and Sanjeev, who had also run away somewhere, were traced and called to report to work. Dhamija was not too keen to drag himself to meet Tanya, but then she was Gautam's girlfriend, which meant relations had to be maintained.

"Tanya-ji, namaste. Sorry ji, but I think I did pass on the paan masala guy's name to you, didn't I? Now, I don't know more than that." What Dhamija did not reveal was that he had actually forgotten about that case, as some juicier case regarding an extramarital fling had taken up his time.

"Arre, I know his name is Nitin. But can you tell me whether he's a married man?"

For a second, Dhamija didn't react. Did that Sowmya lady not tell him that he is her brother? But wait, he himself had some doubts. Oh yes, he did have major doubts. Maybe, he really was Sowmya's husband! Dhamija made a mental note that he should resurrect the case soon, before word of his incompetence got out.

"Haan ji, haan ji, but how does that concern you? I had advised you that very day that Gautam is the man for you," beamed Dhamija in an avuncular way.

"Arre, nahi, please listen to me once. This Nitin, who is your associate Sowmya's husband, does not seem to have a good character. He is openly flirting with my sweet innocent friend. And that is why I feel sorry for Sowmya. Don't you think we should be warning Sowmya about this?"

Dhamija was stunned. That idiot Hari was yet to find how Nitin's photograph landed in that bloody ad. Useless character! This case was going nowhere.

"Haan, haan, you are absolutely right. Bechaari Sowmya should be told about all of this. Now, tell me something more. What does this guy do? Where did he meet your friend?"

Tanya proceeded to recount the longish tale of how Priya and Nitin met and spoke about Nitin's character, or lack thereof, in glowing terms—of course with more embellishments than necessary. Nitin Ranganathan, who up until now had just been an *adh-nanga* paan masala model was a confirmed married rake, all set to ravish the virtues of an innocent, naive Priya.

"Are you sure about this? He does not come across as a scoundrel. *Theek hai, adh-nange ads mein kaam karta hai.* But it is a little difficult to believe that he can be so characterless." Dhamija intervened after patiently listening to Tanya's exaggerated narration.

Tanya insisted that she was telling the truth. And to top that, it was her own precious friend Priya who had seen him with Sowmya and their two boys at the airport. And, for all one knew, he might be a wolf in a sheep's clothing. How can one judge a book by its cover?

Convinced, or rather fed up of this entire case, Dhamija consented to speak with Sowmya. And he did. Sowmya had had to resume her desprate lookout for a domestic help. The one employed from Major Roy Chowdhury's agency had barely lasted a week. She left, stating her complaint clearly, "What is it that we work for? Food. The food in your house is not up to the mark. No fish, no poshto, instead that obnoxious stew-like sambhar and that watery rasam. Can that even be called food?"

Poor Sowmya, in her desperation, now reached out to a whole wide new range of agents, other than the esteemed Major as her search continued. When Dhamija called her, she had been out on the very expedition. She told him that she would come over a bit later in the day. Dhamija, being a rather compassionate man, had issued strict instructions. Sowmya madam had to be welcomed and made comfortable in the office—chai, coffee, juice, samosas and dhoklas had to be served. He felt rather guilty to be the harbinger of such bad news. She was a funny, nice lady, a bit scatter-brained, possibly bossy and chatty, but overall nice. No woman deserved to be told that her husband was a lout. When the hunt for a domestic help proved to be entirely fruitless that day as well, she decided to head over to the Sharp Eye office, where she was welcomed royally.

She did indicate her surprise when she met Dhamija, "What is the news, Dhamija-ji? What are you throwing a party for?"

"Nothing, Ma'am. How have you been?" Dhamija, not used to making small talk, was trying hard.

After chomping down samosas and dhoklas, Sowmya asked him what the matter was. Dhamija turned red, pink and purple and haltingly said: "Ma'am, your husband is not a good man."

"Huh, my husband? What?!! When did you come across him?"

"Ma'am, I am your well-wisher, I think of your well-being. I have been forced to tell you this only after getting a lot of proofs. He is flirting with an office colleague and making all sorts of overtures. That poor scared girl has now complained. I know of just one such instance, we never know how many more such instances might be. He probably needs help."

Sowmya was absolutely dumbfounded. This confident proclamation rendered her speechless. She could not believe her ears. *Her* Bharat cheating on her? That just didn't sound right. A nice man like him would never ever do that. Never. Ever. Just as she was about to issue a quick rebuttal to that irritating detective, Bharat's message popped up on her phone screen, informing her that he won't be home for dinner. It was a message that would have been ignored otherwise, but assumed a momentous proportion, now that seeds of suspicion had been sown in her mind. It also struck her that he had not been home for dinner three times already the past week. What if this detective was telling the truth, she wondered. Bracing herself for the worst, in a small voice, she finally asked Dhamija. Now that Dhamija had found a willing ear, the entire story told to him by Tanya (with further embellishments) was conveyed to her. Poor Sowmya. In a moment, the ground beneath her feet shifted. Bharat, her husband, father to her twins, the jovial, kind guy turned out as a cad of the worst kind, a kind of Jekyll-and-Hyde personality. Here she was suspecting her brother, that poor lad whose only crime seemed to be appearing in some ad, while in reality, it was her husband who was trying to lure an innocent girl into his evil clutches. The rest of the meeting passed off in a blur. With unshed tears blinding her vision, pale and ashen, Sowmya reached home and locked herself up in the room. At home, panic ensued. The twins were distraught; they knew something was wrong with their mother. Latha could not understand what had gone wrong with her daughter. She had never seen her feisty daughter in such a state before. Extremely worried when Sowmya did not come out even after an hour, she called Bharat, and he immediately rushed home.

And then hell broke loose. Bharat Ramamohan did not know what hit him. He found himself left all alone, with his wife walking out on him, taking the kids and her mother along with her. His sweet mother-in-law had tried to intervene, to understand what exactly had gone wrong. But Sowmya would not explain. She wanted out, a clean-cut, a divorce. Bharat could not understand what he had done or not done. In the end, feeling foolish and frustrated, he just shut up and watched as his life, once comfortable and settled, crumbled into pieces right in front of his eyes.

# CHAPTER 13

Meanwhile, Nitin had been having a worrisome day. Too many calls from Vinod and planned onsite meetings related to other projects meant that he couldn't head over to the Kintech office, while he had been looking forward to it. The meetings took much too long and the day was almost over. He had just resigned himself to the fact that his grand "woo the girl" plan would have to wait for another day, and now he had started contemplating Plan B. Should he text her? Call her?

His mother had been frantically calling him to summon him home at once. Since his mother had not said a word but sounded so worried and shaken, Nitin was tense by the time he reached home.

Adding to this worry was the dreary silence. His normally boisterous sister was sprawled out, Meena Kumari style, on the couch, mindlessly changing channels as the kids played quietly near her. It was his mother's face that underlined the gravity of the situation. She was wan and pale.

"Talk to her, Nitin. *Pesame irrukura* (She isn't saying a word)."

"Sowmu, *enna aachi* (What happened)?"

It was then that he noticed the two suitcases kept near the door. Had Sowmya walked out on Bharat? But theirs was a decent marriage; Bharat seemed to dote on his sister, even though she was exasperating; he used to indulge each and every whim of hers, without a murmur. The man even took a pay cut and moved back to India some years back, all because she was homesick and wanted to return! What was going on?

"Sowmya, what is going on? Look, we are with you and will support you. But you need to tell us what has happened?"

Sowmya, who had been unnaturally silent till now, suddenly reacted strongly. She became uncontrollably hysterical, wailing and crying, thankfully remembering to shut the twins' ears in a clumsy way as she ranted about the cheating, rakish, profligate Bharat.

Nitin was shocked. *Are women generally insane—especially the loud, noisy types?*

"Bharat?! Sowmya, are you okay? He is a loving dad and an equally loving husband."

"I know, that's what I always believed him to be. But now I get to know he is just the opposite. He has been carrying on with some girl in his office. Imagine. If he were having a midlife crisis, or whatever they have at his age, couldn't he have done something else? He could've coloured his hair, or maybe started a business! Instead, this! And he even berated me!" wailed Sowmya.

"Berated you? How?"

"He told me that *I* was stepping out of line and that I should start getting looking for productive ways to get busy! And he added that all these yoga and other classes and associating with those jobless Belvedere Park middle-aged ladies has made me go mad!

"Hmm, let me speak to him."

"No way. I am done. I am getting a divorce."

Realizing that saying anything more would trigger yet another knee-jerk reaction, Nitin kept quiet and started playing with his nephews. His heart went out for them. No kid deserved to see such ugly scenes. The evening passed by, a huge dark shadow looming large on the entire family.

The next few days ushered in subtle changes. Priya's resolve at avoiding Nitin at work and lunch were proving to be rather successful, mostly because the said gentleman was nowhere to be seen. Priya's achievement was that she held her tongue and curiosity under check. She did not ask Urvashi, with whom she had become rather friendly, though she did came close to quite a few times, especially by the end of the week when she overheard a conversation, in snatches and bits. As she was walking towards Vishal's cubicle, a spot she had started dropping by more frequently than before, only to check the status of some project, Urvashi and Anuj were in a serious conversation. Urvashi was speaking, and Anuj and Abhishek were listening, spell-bound. All Priya could manage to hear was "poor man … it is going to be a divorce … the poor poor kids … Nitin must be so shattered … he dotes on them."

Her heart did all sorts of double takes. At first, it sank despairingly, but then there was this hope, weird little thing. Was Nitin getting a divorce? Did he realize he had fallen irrevocably in love with her and hence couldn't carry on the sham of a marriage? Was that what it was? Could she hope for something more? The more her mind fled in such directions, thinking up preposterous thoughts, and throwing up images of a big house, two kids, cats and all, she wanted to throw up and wail.

Then better sense prevailed. She calmly sat down and thought why she was behaving like a drama queen. Since she got no answers for this profound question, she shifted her focus to whatever she was supposed to be doing. Damn it. Tanya was right. Instead of being a nerdy, studious idiot in school and college, one who would only focus on misplaced priorities such as education, she should have dated. But no, she spent those days pining for that useless dolt Karthik. Damn him. What a colossal idiot she was now at twenty-six. She really did need a shrink after all. She knew it was time to check with Tanya about what should be done under such changed circumstances. Her chain of thoughts started taking over once again. *You duffer. What changed circumstances. He could be divorcing his wife for any reason. He may not even be interested in you. Can you please stop?*

As this mental dialogue went on and on, leaving her exhausted, Priya decided it was high time she took charge of her life. And the first thing she planned to do was to apply for a week's leave and go home to Bengaluru. Sushil, noticing that Priya had been quieter and more distracted than usual, approved the leave immediately, urging her to go home right away. This unexpected avuncular behaviour from the dreaded boss left her feeling worse. Was he planning to fire her? Had her work quality suffered the past few weeks? Damn Nitin. Damn Karthik. Convinced that she urgently needed help to manage the mental turmoil she was experiencing, or at least a cup of coffee with her best friend, Priya left early and surprised Tanya at the Sunlit Path.

Over a cup of coffee, Priya told Tanya about her new plan. She would now take a break, go home in Bengaluru, meet her parents, aunts, uncles, cousins and all. She would also tell her parents to look for a good, well-educated, 'unmarried' South Indian boy whom she could meet during this break (if at all any were left in India and not all had migrated to Silicon Valley).

Tanya, overjoyed at her friend sounding her usual sensible self once again, was of course encouraging. She also smartly suggested that since Gautam moved around in these intellectual circles with his quizzing friends, he would know some eligible guys too for Priya—an idea that was much welcomed by the latter. Moreover, the Mahaquiz was due next week, the grand one hosted by Karnataka Quizzing Association (KQA). Maybe Priya would meet someone there.

"Arre, no, Nitin might be there. Bad idea."

"I don't think so. He is getting a divorce. He isn't even coming to office these days," rued a sad Priya.

"Divorce? So soon? When did this happen?" Tanya was genuinely surprised. In her zeal to save all womankind from the notorious Nitin, she had not realized that it could have such serious repercussion in Sowmya's and Nitin's lives. Had she exaggerated a bit too much while speaking to Dhamija? So far, that Nitin guy hadn't really done anything. Yes, his intentions were bad, but does that warrant a divorce? Don't all men, single or married, ogle at other women? They do. This fellow just got too friendly with her friend—maybe not in a touchy-feely way but otherwise. Had Tanya meddled too much? All this should never have been told told to Priya.

When Nitin came back to Kintech office, after a week-long absence spent in getting used to his new life, Priya was nowhere to be seen. Nitin's schedule was different now. With his sister, now usually lying sprawled on the couch, dabbing her eyes often, gorging on ice cream or reading, the upbringing of her two boys had completely fallen on their mother, a new domestic help, Monju, (God bless Major Roy Chowdhury; and this Bengali lady was okay with eating watery rasam and obnoxious sambhars) and Nitin. If Latha Ranganathan and Monju had taken charge of getting the boys' breakfast and tiffin boxes ready in time for school, it was Nitin's responsibility to drop them to school and pick them up and then take them for their taekwondo and football classes later in the evening. The changed circumstances meant that work and other pastimes took a backseat, at least for now. Not that he minded. This was indeed good practice for his future life (the one with the big house, two kids, dog and all). Plus, he was genuinely concerned about his sister and brother-in-law and the mess they found themselves in.

Mr Ranganathan had since been apprised of this new development and while he had offered to fly down to Gurugram, he had been persuaded for now to stay put in Malleshwaram. Latha was worried that her plants would dry up. He could come down, in case their mad daughter decided to actually follow through with her divorce threat. He listened to the suggestion. Moreover, he secretly believed that only scoundrels and crazy people lived in Delhi-NCR and thus was rather happy tending to Latha's plants and attending *sewai*s (poojas) and *katcheri*s (concerts) at the nearby Venugopalaswamy Temple. It is also true that he knew his daughter was a little hysterical, a bit crazy (just like his own perima, Ranganayakamma). He knew she would come to her senses and reconcile with Bharat, and even if she didn't, it was perfectly alright. He was really not that bothered, unlike Latha. Nitin, meanwhile, had been holding secret consultations with both his parents, following which he went and met Bharat. He was shocked to see how worried and serious his otherwise usually jovial brother-in-law seemed.

"Nitin, I do not know what she is going on and on about. I am supposedly having an affair with some girl in my office. I asked her who this girl was. She said she did not know. Imagine. She hears something from someone and has walked out on me."

Poor Nitin knew not what to say. Should he defend his sister? Should he sympathize with Bharat? How is one supposed to behave, when stuck in between a warring couple? He just shut up and let Bharat continue.

"Stupid decision to leave her job. I told her a hundred times not to. But no, when does she ever listen? She wanted a break from office politics, or so she said. Instead, she runs around, pursuing everything from yoga to pilates—there was this classical music phase also in between—and last I heard, she and those crazy women she hangs around with wanted to learn something obscure. Jobless women, I tell you! And did she tell you? The last month or so, she was assisting some detective. I must have been mad to have married this crazy woman. How are the boys? I miss them."

Nitin's mediation plans had to be terminated. He understood his brother-in-law's frustration completely and he too personally believed that his sister was acting like a crazy woman. Bharat was no lying, cheating profligate (*aah that word*)! He started wondering how Priya was doing. He had heard no news about her. She was simply nowhere to be seen. Should he call? Or text? Unlike Priya, who had had issues of her own and could not ask Urvashi, Nitin did not have such qualms. After asking around, checking up with Vishal and Urvashi, separately of course, he found out that Priya had gone on leave, back to home in Bengaluru. Was she alright? Her parents? Should he ask Gautam or Tanya? No, that may seem strange. He had hardly informed them why he had suddenly dropped off the quizzing radar. While he did not ask Gautam about Priya, he did however touch base with him to check on the quizzing calendar for later in the year. He also apologized for disappearing without prior notice, stating personal issues as the reason. Gautam commiserated with Nitin and offered to lend a shoulder, over some drinks. It was an offer that Nitin gladly took up, adding he would call him soon. After all, one could not blame this young man. For all the practice it offered him, minding two kids most of the time and listening to a wailing woman (who had now taken to singing sad Tamil songs, like '*Naane naana yaaro thaana*', in a slightly off-key note, even though it hardly fit her situation) could be very exasperating. The men, unknown to Tanya, made plans for catching up.

# CHAPTER 14

Meanwhile, in Bengaluru, Priya was being pampered by her indulgent Appa, Amma, Paati and the rest of her family members. While to the world (read Tanya), she was determined to carry on with her resolve, but she was definitely struggling. The first two days of the holiday indeed did her good. She caught up on her sleep, gorged on home-made food, caught up with aunts, uncles and some cousins. But that was it. Third day onwards, with no productive work to concentrate on, her mind kept going back to Nitin. He was so nice, caring and attentive, and that too not just with her. But what was that silly status she saw on Facebook the other day? *The love of your life need not be the love in your life*. Was that her sign? Were they star-crossed lovers? As she started thinking about the love stories of Romeo–Juliet and Heer–Ranjha, thankfully rationality interjected. What an idiot she was, and it was that Karthik's fault. Look, what that dalliance has made her—a neurotic, pathetic woman. She should create a voodoo doll in his likeness and start poking needles into it—that would serve that jerk right. For all her destructive tendencies, she suddenly realized that she had no clue how Karthik looked now. She had not seen him for about seven to eight years. Should she stalk him on Facebook? Bah, a ridiculous idea! She needed to get over this Nitin character and not start obsessing *again* about that Karthik. But why would Nitin, such a nice and affectionate man even think of cheating on his wife? She couldn't help but wonder whether it was because she herself was so charming? *Bullshit*. Maybe that wife wasn't a good lady, maybe she was a nag, a dominating woman? Maybe she cheated on Nitin first and maybe she is carrying her paramour's child, forcing Nitin to try to cheat on her, purely out of revenge. And since he was too honourable to actually cheat on his wife, maybe he was now getting divorced? As her imagination started running wild in all directions, she realized she was beginning to sound more like Tanya and thus desperately needed to get back to work. She pulled out her office laptop and started working, checking emails, and so on. Should she just cut short her vacation and return?

Her father, P.R. Kaushik, noticing her restlessness, tried to probe. Was everything alright in Delhi? Priya of course replied in the affirmative. While nothing was wrong per se, she was starting to feel rather lonely in life. She told her parents that she was finally amenable to marriage. She did not have any one in mind (*such a liar).* Her parents were surprised at her sudden change of mind, but decided to explore further. As they were discussing her plans, Amma dropped a bombshell. She was told that her childhood *friend* Karthik was back home? The poor guy is divorced. He met us at the temple the other day and was asking about you. That was it! *Paavam, my foot!* Within minutes, Priya's mind was made up—her leave cancelled, she was back in Delhi in a jiffy.

**Later that day**

"Priya, what happened, why are you back so soon? That Sharma called you back from vacation?" screeched Tanya when Priya called her from the airport.

"Na re, will tell you when we meet, okay?"

"Call me when you land in Delhi. Kiran aunty is here at the store. I am leaving now."

Over yet another cup of coffee, Priya confided in Tanya. She had not been able to get Nitin off her mind. She wondered whether Tanya or Gautam had heard from him. Work was proving to be her only panacea. She also told Tanya about Karthik, and that he was back, divorced, and even asking about her!

"What?! No, no, no. Priya Kaushik, it took you three long years to regain your composure and go back to being yourself. No Karthik."

"I know, baba. But I just had a scary scary thought … Karthik was divorced, Nitin will soon be divorced; now should I not be picking a known devil instead of an unknown angel? Imagine, I rushed to Delhi because I was so close to thinking about Karthik again. I took the first flight I could catch. Amma and Appa were surprised. There's no way I'll meet that jerk ever again. What if I ended up stabbing him! Tanu, you should be proud of me. I have asked Amma and Appa to find me a good boy based out of India preferably. Good, no?"

"Oh, yes, darling, that's the spirit."

Feeling much better after this heart-to-heart talk, Priya was looking forward to getting back to work the following day. Of course, he-who-shall-not-be-thought-of, the one with the good looks and bad character, might just be there. But then, what is life without challenges!

***

In an upscale condominium in Gurugram, Latha Ranganathan was slowly but surely running out of patience. In her mid-sixties, Latha, normally of an amiable disposition, was a devout woman who gained much solace and pleasure in her set daily routine involving prayers, plants and music. When she came to Gurugram a little less than a month ago, it was with an express purpose to speak to and influence her son to get married. She certainly had not envisaged turning into a full-time nanny-cum-housekeeper for her daughter! And though she loved her children and grandchildren, she was definitely getting bugged now.

The more she reflected upon the past month, she despaired. The more she observed her children and thought about what they had got into, she panicked and worried. Her daughter, eccentric, boisterous and flighty, had now turned into a drama queen. And that boy had started appearing in near-naked advertisements, clearly displaying a streak of exhibitionism. How on earth did such a thing even happen! Neither she nor her husband ever promoted such tendencies. It must be that Peri Ma, Ranganayakamma. After having found out the root cause for these eccentricities in her children, Latha decided to do what she knew best: handle both of them. To begin with, Sowmya was the one who needed some handling first.

Sowmya's melodramatic episode, wherein she sat in front of the TV, lying down on the couch, with bowls of ice cream, was cut short as her mother went all ballistic. Latha Ranganathan used to be a strict mother once upon a time—and both her kids were terrified when she went off in that vein. All it took was one shout, and Sowmya was back. Moreover, she had started getting quite bored. It is not always that one gets a sudden break from one's responsibilities and can loll around in front of the TV without being questioned, and attracting sympathy at the same time. It had been perfect for a while. So once past the initial shock and heartbreak, she had started enjoying the state of affairs. It had been fun. Monju did most of the work and Amma looked after the boys. Why, even Nitin had been there—running around and doing everything to make her happy. But to her own surprise, Sowmya had slowly started getting bored. How much TV could one watch? How much ice cream could one eat? There were also these interesting developments on her condominium's WhatsApp group. Oh, how she missed her yoga and pilates sessions! How she missed Belvedere Park and her lovely friends! Not that she would ever admit this to anyone, but she missed Bharat too. After the initial shock and rage had subsided, Sowmya thought about what Dhamija had said—that her husband had begun to get too friendly with someone in his office. Heck, since when did good friendship become synonymous with love affairs in real life? Had Dhamija been reading too many film magazines? Moreover, no names or concrete source had been given by Dhamija. Was he just fibbing? Finally, many weeks after the entire drama had unfolded, Sowmya started thinking.

Sowmya pulled herself away from the couch, mainly because Latha was giving her *that* look, the one that never failed to terrify her and get her to behave. Since age was just a number and nothing really ever changed, the look worked even now!

Within an hour, Sowmya had landed up at the Dhamija office, without a prior appointment, rousing the sleepy office into immediate action. Dhamija, who had been dozing rather peacefully in his room, woke up at the sudden commotion outside. "Hari, Sanjeev, *abe gadhon, kar kya rahe ho?*"

As he straightened his kurta, ready to go and check on the state of his office, he saw Sowmya walk in.

"Namaste Dhamija-ji. How are you?

"*Arre, Madam-ji app*?" Dhamija couldn't believe his eyes. He had expected that a woman who had been told that her husband was a jerk would be sad and weepy. But the woman in front of him looked as charged as before, and to top that, she even looked better. Regular sleep, rest and all that ice cream seemed to have done Sowmya a world of good.

"Your face seems to be glowing."

"Ji?"

Was that a glow on her face, Dhamija wondered. No, it was just the light falling on her face, tinging it with a golden hue!

"How have you been? Please tell me how I may help you."

Sowmya delved straight to the point, as always. "I want to meet her, Dhamija-ji?"

"But who?"

"Dhamija-ji, the one you were telling me about."

Dhamija had no clue as to whom she was referring to. He sat, gawking at her, rubbing his eyes. The woman looked peaceful and happy. Is that how all women look when they shoo their husbands away? Would Anita also look so happy and relaxed? Dhamija suddenly got very worried and made a mental note to be extra nice to his wife.

"Dhamija-ji, you told me that my husband was having an affair, right? Who is the woman? I want to meet her."

"Oh, ma'am, I do not know who the woman is. But I will introduce you to the lady who told me all about your husband's affair, okay?

"Ji, I'll be waiting."

"Do you want to meet her today?"

Sowmya just glared. She wanted to get done with this meeting. Dhamija excused himself and called Tanya, who was sitting in the Sunlit Path, immersed in a world filled with swashbuckling knights rescuing damsels in distress!

It took a while for her to come back to this present world and understand what Dhamija was saying. "Achchha, you are that Dhamija-ji! You want me to come to your office? Why? What is it that you want from me?"

"Madam, what nonsense is this?" said the shocked Dhamija. No one had ever doubted this character. *Girls these days. All of them are crazy. They shouldn't be allowed to go anywhere by themselves. I should keep an eye on what Sanjana is doing,* thought Dhamija as he worried about his twelve-year-old pre-teen.

"Oh, ho, Dhamija-ji, sorry, sorry. I was feeling a little lost. Now please tell me. You would like me to come to your office? New development? Ji, fine. Will be there."

Dhamija had not told Tanya why he was calling her to his office. To her surprise, she saw Sowmya sitting and browsing through a film magazine, reading an interview about good friends. Meanwhile, Sowmya was busy thinking about Bharat and his "good friend".

"Ma'am, meet Tanya Grover."

"Hi, I am Sowmya Bharat," she said, extending a hand for Tanya to shake, while observing her intensely. The girl looked sweet. Introductions done, Dhamija-ji left the room, preferring to let the women discuss whatever they had to. He was also worried that he would get caught right in the middle of a cat-fight. Contrary to Dhamija's worry, the conversation between Sowmya and Tanya never deteriorated into any kind of tussle or argument. They hit it off rather well, both liking each other at first sight. The tone of the conversation was rather amiable.

"You know my husband?"

"Hmm, kind of. I met him a couple of months back. My best friend works in the same office as he."

"Ah, your best friend is the one then. What happened?"

"From what I know, they work together. Your husband started getting too friendly, in fact started crossing the line too. My friend is an innocent girl—I won't let her get involved with a married man. Dhamija-ji is kind of known to me. I told him to warn you. No serious affair yet, but you see, once a cheat, always a cheat. I wanted to warn you."

Sowmya, touched at the reply, got emotional. "I don't have a sister. But seeing you, I feel I do. You are like my own sister. Thank you so much. I did need to know about my husband and his doings."

"What are you planning to do now?"

"I walked out the very day I got to know about it. I am living with my brother for now. I might file for a divorce. I don't know. It is so heartbreaking," Sowmya replied, bursting into tears. Seeing her howl, poor Tanya, one with a sentimental heart as always, eyes moist with tears, pulled her into a warm hug.

As the women hugged and dabbed their eyes, Sowmya said, "You may not be my sister, but you definitely can be my sister-in-law. Are you married? Grover, na? Punjabi. Doesn't matter. Appa and Amma will ultimately come around."

"What? No! no. Please. I am not married, but I have a boyfriend."

"Hmm, okay then. I was just trying."

"I don't mind. Please let me know in case you need me to do anything. I would love to help. If we women do not stand for each other, who will?"

Expressing such solidarity for each other and every other woman in the city, country and globe, Sowmya and Tanya exchanged numbers, made plans to meet, and then bid adieu. Tanya came back home feeling horrible. What sort of a jerk was this Nitin? Who could even think of leaving such a nice lady? Men were horrid creatures really. Here was this woman who has borne this cad two lovely kids, and there he was flirting with an innocent, naive girl. Do they not have a conscience?

The more Tanya thought about it, the more she felt that she was getting closer to her calling. She wanted to help distressed women across the city get away from the vicious clutches of the horrid men in their lives. There must be some Mahila Mukti Kendra nearby where she could go and contribute. She decided to check with Gautam. But first, she needed to tackle the issue about Sowmya's love life. In her new-found zeal, Tanya decided to help her find a good lawyer. She did not have to find much, as one messaged her just then.

Unlike Priya whose school crush had turned completely sour, Tanya's hadn't. Arvind Arora did not even know that Tanya Grover had had a crush on him that lasted precisely two days. The third day, unknown to him, Arvind had serious competition from another guy, who eventually won, sweeping Tanya off her feet. Arvind was relegated to being a good friend and remained one of her close friends since. As she saw his message flash on her phone screen, she remembered that he was indeed a hotshot lawyer. Corporate or criminal or family law—what did it matter? Even if not able to take on the case, he would at least be able to recommend a good lawyer who could help Sowmya file for a divorce. Messages exchanged with Arvind Arora and Sowmya in question, Tanya felt contented and happy. She was doing the world some good!

Arvind Arora turned out to be a corporate lawyer, but just as Tanya had expected, he did refer her to a couple of lawyers who specialized in family law. With all the necessary information in hand, Tanya called Sowmya later that evening to understand how she wished to proceed.

By now, Sowmya had started feeling jittery about her decision. It seemed she did not really wish to divorce Bharat. Heck, she loved him, despite everything he had been up to. He was after all the father of her children, those lovely lads ... one can't dump the father of one's kids just like that, no? How could she do this to dear old Bharat? There is something wilful about pig-headedness. You know you are about to commit a huge blunder but you shall not reconsider your decision. This is what had happened to Sowmya. However, despite all the inner conflict and struggle, Sowmya steeled herself and told Tanya that she would meet the lawyer in question. For that, she meekly requested Tanya to accompany her for moral strength. Thus, plans were made. It was decided that Tanya would drop by and pick up Sowmya from her apartment and go with her to Manesar, which is where the lawyer had set up shop.

# CHAPTER 15

**A few days later**

To everyone's surprise, including Monju's, Sowmya was up and about early, active and bustling around the morning she was to meet the lawyer. She even offered to drop her kids to school—though the kids and their uncle shot down the offer. Nitin and the boys had a secret. The indulgent uncle would get them an ice cream daily before dropping them off, something neither Sowmya nor Latha knew about. Had they known, Nitin would have had it. But for now, the boys' secret was safe. "Amma, Nitin, I am planning to file for a divorce," announced Sowmya as soon as Nitin returned after dropping the boys.

"Are you sure, Sowmya?"

"Yes, Nitin. No point going on like this."

"Have you found a lawyer?" asked her mother, trying to assess the seriousness of this sudden proclamation.

"My friend Tanya has. She is coming to take me to this lawyer in Manesar."

Nitin, allergic to that name, reacted, "Who is this friend Tanya? I haven't heard of her before. Have we met her?"

"Nitin, my brother, the way I do not know all your friends, you do not know all of my friends," glared Sowmya, as she lolled around, turning the pages of the newspaper, and flipping through the TV channels simultaneously.

Nitin shut up but couldn't quell the uneasy feeling he had. He really did not like that name. And if all Tanyas were like the Tanya he knew, God help the world.

One can only imagine his shock when the doorbell rang and he opened the door.

"You?"

"What are you doing here?"

"I live here. You know Sowmya?"

"She is a good friend. Now will you let me in? And tell me, why are you here?"

"Excuse me, this is my house."

As Tanya walked in, continuing to glare at Nitin, she was confused. Did Sowmya not tell her that she had walked out on her husband and that she was living with her brother? The one she almost tried to pair Tanya with yesterday. What was Nitin doing here? Was he her brother?

"You… are…. Sowmya's brother—hi Sowmya, all ready?"

"Yes," replied both Sowmya and Nitin.

"Do you know each other?" asked Sowmya, her matchmaking dreams once again coming to the fore.

"Kind of," muttered Nitin.

"Tanya, please meet my brother Nitin. He is a wonderful guy. Any girl would be so lucky to have him in her life. Think about what I told you yesterday."

"What did you tell her yesterday, Sowmya?" Nitin interjected quickly. Both these women were notorious when it came to making mischief.

"Uh, oh, nothing really. I like her. I like you. How would it be if both of you, you know, got together? I was just wondering."

"No," the two of them screamed in unison.

Tanya stood there, in shock, as if the ground had been swept away from under her feet. This was most confusing. Why had that Hari told her that Nitin was Sowmya's husband? Arre, he was not even married. Oh God, in her zeal to protect Priya, she had sabotaged her happy ending. What about poor Sowmya? Who the hell was Sowmya's husband? What had she done? She felt horrible, utterly terrible. What a mess she had created. How on earth was she to rectify it?

The rest of the day passed by in a complete haze. Tanya hardly registered what was discussed or spoken about at the lawyer's. She felt utterly miserable and extremely foolish as she tried to come up with solutions to the problem. *No, no, do not think up any more things, you idiot. You have gone and messed up this dear sweet lady's life. Go back home and talk to Gautam, dad or just about anyone.*

Tanya wouldn't have fretted that much had she known what was going on inside Sowmya's mind. Her pig-headedness may have got her up to this point. As she heard the lawyer speak, she started rethinking. Bharat, but for these *good friends*, had always been a great husband. Kind, loving and adjusting—who else would have put up with her so patiently all these years?

At the end of the meeting, when Sowmya did not fix a date for a follow-up meeting, Tanya was relieved. Knowing that time was of essence, Tanya decided to act and proceeded immediately to Dhamija's office. After all, wasn't it there that she had got hold of this information? So, why should she be the one feeling so guilty? Dhamija and his useless team should be held responsible. Thank heavens, there was still time.

Of late, the summer months had been taking a toll on Dhamija. Business was slow and the few cases they had were also piling up. It was too hot to go out snooping and looking around. Anita would not let him stay home. Dhamija was forced to come to his office, where he could barely take a nap despite the latest additions of a TV and an air conditioner. When Sanvi informed Dhamija that Tanya Grover had come to meet him, without an appointment, he felt even more hassled. Ever since she had told him about Nitin being Sowmya's husband and made him do the dirty job of passing on that information to poor Sowmya, he had been perturbed. It just did not feel right—no, no, anyone who worked in *ashleel* ads was definitely capable of such antics. It was just that the case had been solved too easily. Tanya's arrival again, even after her case had been solved, portended something worse.

Tanya barged straight in and went on the offensive.

"Dhamija-ji, Gautam had told me that you are the best detective in Delhi. But your team has turned out to be very useless."

"Ji, ma'am? What are you saying? Hasn't your case been solved already? Arre, weren't you the one who looked into who the paan masala guy was?"

"Nonsense. I came to know about him from your people!"

"What? What is it you are saying, ma'am? Who are these people you are talking about?"

That very moment, Hari walked in with two chilled glasses of nimbu pani along with a plate of sad-looking oily samosas, and laid it on the table.

Tanya pointed to him and gesticulating wildly said, "It's he! He was the one who told me that Nitin was Sowmya's husband!"

Hari was dumbfounded, his mouth and eyes open.

"You dumb idiot person! What crap do you go around telling people?!" screeched Dhamija, demanding an explanation.

Hari stood still, transfixed, not knowing what to say. He had no idea what his crazy boss and the crazier lady were shouting about. "But what have I done?"

"It was because of you that Sowmya ma'am was getting a divorce!" yelled an agitated Tanya.

"Because of me? That's not possible, I have not done anything!"

Five minutes later, a foggy picture began to emerge. Had anyone told him that Nitin was Sowmya's husband? No. Hari had just assumed. His logic was that: no sane woman would keep a near-naked picture of some man, certainly not that of her own brother; so the man must be her husband. But did Hari look into how and where that ad was shot? No, no one knew about it till date. The only thing Hari was able to find out was that a Bhojpuri film-maker was looking for hero. He wondered whether he should give Nitin's phone number to this man?

Dhamija had had enough. Shooing Hari to the back of his office, he sat down, inhaling deeply. This was indeed a mess. Poor Sowmya-ji and poor Sowmya-ji's husband.

"What do we do now, Dhamija-ji?"

"What do you mean by 'what do we do now'? We will have to talk to Sowmya madam."

Dhamija once again called Sowmya requesting her to kindly come down to his office at the earliest. It was a matter of life and death, he said. He sent Hari and Sanjeev with strict instructions to bring kachoris (samosas that day were not good) and gulab jamuns, and hot jalebis also, if available.

Sowmya had a sinking feeling as she walked in. Both Tanya and Dhamija were there, speechless and scared. And the delicacies on the table gave her a sense of creepy deja vu.

"Dhamija-ji, what has happened now? Tell me quickly. Tanya, how come you too are here? What has Bharat done now?

"Bharat, that's what his name is," Dhamija kept quiet as Tanya paused trying to phrase and frame her thoughts. Since keeping quiet and thinking were cumbersome activities for her, she quickly recovered and started: "Sowmya, I am very sorry; no, we are very sorry," glaring at Dhamija who picked up the cue and also nodded, apologetically.

"What has happened? Has Bharat converted to Islam? To marry your innocent friend? Has he already remarried?" Sowmya was now visibly panicky.

"No, madam, it is not like that. You please have some nimbu paani."

"Actually, it was our fault. We assumed Nitin was your husband," admitted Tanya sheepishly.

"What?!" Sowmya paused for a minute, before launching into a tirade. "Bharat is nowhere in the picture?! Dhamija-ji, you claim to be such a great detective. Is this how you solve cases? Believe anything and everything someone tells you!

"And you? You assumed? You see two people together and believe that they are married?! How old are you? What on earth have I done! Poor Bharat."

"Ma'am, we are very sorry. This idiot Hari is the one who is behind this utter confusion. Tanya ma'am was also asking about the same paan masala ad. That idiot ended up telling her that Nitin is your husband. I should have checked. Please forgive me."

Sowmya had calmed down a bit and then as the full import of the situation dawned upon her, she burst into laughter, intermingled with tears of relief.

"Oh, that ad. And Nitin is flirting with your friend? Who is she?"

"Um ... hmm, flirting is a strong word. He has been showing interest in her. Of course, she has been rebuffing him, thanks to this whole confusion. She thinks he is married, na. She saw you with him, apparently."

"Have I met her? What is her name?"

"Priya."

"Pretty Priya, of course. I met her at the airport. Aha! So my brother is interested in her. Good you told me this. We need to see what can be done about this, once I set my house in order," said Sowmya, as she finally smiled, indicating that she was now feeling better.

Dhamija was staring. Women were strange creatures. Such a major goof-up, almost disastrous, one that nearly wrecked her home, and yet this woman was charting marriage plans for her brother! As the women left, Dhamija took matters into his hand and blasted idiotic Hari yet again, though to no avail. Hari continued to gawk at him, mouth open, firm in his belief that his boss was crazy.

Five minutes after leaving Dhamija's office, Sowmya's euphoria had subsided. She was now nervous. What was she to do now? How could she face Bharat? Her entire reaction, on hindsight, now seemed extremely hasty. She had not given him a chance to explain. He did not even know what he had done. Poor guy, no wonder he was so shaken. Was there any way she could right this wrong? She had wronged him grievously; she wondered how he was doing and coping with the turn of events. *Was he eating well*—but before she could get more of such thoughts, her conscience interjected. *Lady, you know well. He must be happily eating what the cook would have prepared!* On second thoughts, should she go over to his office and apologize?

Should she send him some flowers and cake?! She picked the first option and landed up at Bharat Ramamohan's fifteenth-floor office in the busy, hi-tech Cyber City area of Gurugram.

Considering that this was the first time she was entering his office, and that too at an hour when most offices were already wrapping up for the day, Sowmya had a slightly tough time getting to the fifteenth floor. The man was not answering his phone and his secretary, Sudha, a matronly middle-aged woman, was not available either. She would have left by now. As Sowmya walked into Bharat's plush corner office, unannounced, the poor man, whose days had been stressful—thanks to a high-pressured job and the antics of a deranged wife—looked fed-up. "Sowmya, what a surprise. Have you come here to hand over the divorce papers?"

Sowmya knew she was in trouble. When Bharat is miffed, he would be sarcastic. As she kept quiet, looking rather sheepish, the man was definitely surprised. He knew that his wife must have come to her senses, else she would have been shouting her head off by now.

"Sorry, Bharat. You weren't flirting with anyone ..."

"Huh, wait, you walked out on me because you thought I was flirting with someone? That was what this was all about? Not even an affair? Flirting? How much of an idiot are you?!"

"Well, kind of ... but it is not so simple as it sounds. But you didn't know my reason?" Sowmya asked, feeling very foolish, as she thought about it harder.

"I would have known had you told me, instead of creating all that drama. Are you seriously that stupid?!"

"I have come here to apologize, not get insulted."

"Why should I make it any easier for you, Sowmu? I am peeved and very hurt. This is unacceptable. We have been married so long. Do you not know me at all? And now you say you walked out because you thought I was flirting with someone. What an immature, irresponsible idiot! What kind of example are we setting for the boys? How many times do I have to tell you? You need to get a job. All this time on hand and the crazy company you keep is driving you nuts. And which one of those crazy women do I need to thank for this latest excitement in my life? Whose brilliant idea was it? Walk out on husband because one of them saw me smile at some random woman? Alisha? Sumedha?"

"Arre, I know you don't like Alisha or Sumedha, but Bharat, they had nothing to do with this terrible misunderstanding. It is a long story. Can we please go home now?"

# CHAPTER 16

The drama-filled Ranaganathan and Ramamohan households slowly returned to normality. Nitin had his home and schedule back to himself, giving him the mental bandwidth to now pursue his "woo the girl" project with a renewed vigour. As the Sowmya–Bharat drama had intensified at home, Nitin's appearances at the KintechLearning office had become rather limited. He had started making an appearance only when absolutely necessary, which meant that he hadn't seen Priya much over these weeks. He could easily count on his fingers the number of times he had been there recently. Yes, he was keeping count. The meetings were fleeting, too short and to the point, even more so because Priya was no longer involved with the Parity Global project. In fact, she hardly came to that corner now. Most of these meetings were lately being held at the CCD coffee corner. He had tried to approach Priya to strike a conversation, but she always came across as intimidating, his hopes being nipped in the bud.

Priya had been progressing rather well with her resolution of staying away from Nitin. The fact that he was mostly out of sight and not in office helped immensely. The few times they met had been too short to even be considered. There was a sense of lacuna each time. She wanted to talk to him, only to check on his well-being because he looked so forlorn. The divorce was definitely proving to be hard on him, she guessed. But then her saner mind, the one that had made her announce to the parents that she wished to get married, intervened. She decided to hold back herself once again. Once in a while, she would try eavesdropping on Urvashi's phone calls, or conversations—just to get an inkling of what was happening to Nitin. But all of that was out of genuine concern for him, nothing else. She had no wish to get involved with a married man—be it Nitin or that jackass Karthik.

Ever since she had given her assent to her parents to officially proceed with groom hunting, the Kaushiks had been busy. Contact with relatives, far and near, had been re-established; word had been spread among neighbours and friends. All the *vadhyar mamas* (priests) at the nearby temples had been informed. The Kaushiks had even started attending every function in town, even if they were taking place in Whitefield, be it an engagement or an *upanayanam* (sacred thread ceremony). After all, they had an uphill task ahead of them of finding a highly educated, good South Indian boy from their community based out of India—a rare species! A list was duly prepared, relevant details, like biodata, horoscopes and photographs, procured and emailed to Priya within no time. Priya opened the email with much trepidation. One never knew what kind of men could be lurking behind the seemingly perfect photographs and biodata. She knew Amma would expect an answer without much delay.

Priya was looking forward to Tanya's return later in the week. After doing her bit in helping the Sowmya–Bharat reconciliation, Tanya had had to rush to Amritsar. A grandaunt had passed away and she was expected to be there with the Grovers for the cremation and subsequent rituals. In all the chaos, the 'Nitin-is-single-hallelujah' revelation had slipped her mind. And when she did remember, she felt a bit too guilty about causing all the confusion, and decided to come clean to Priya once they would be face-to-face. Meanwhile, Priya decided to wait until the weekend to go through the profiles. However, that decision was to be rather a short-lived one.

The next day, Nitin went to the office in a happy frame of mind. Not that Priya knew about this; she was having a rather chaotic day chasing some deliverables for the oil and natural gas client who had become extremely demanding of late. To her absolute surprise, in fact shock, she found him seated in her cabin a little while after lunch. His unannounced presence shook her. "You are back? Havent seen you around much these days," she muttered, fumbling for words. Her mind was racing. *Idiot, don't gawk. You need to speak.*

Nitin did not seem to mind the awkwardness, and he interacted with her in a friendly and warm manner. He seemed genuinely interested in finding out how she had been and what had been happening in her life the past month. *Why is he being so nice to me? Or maybe his divorce has come through? Should he not show some remorse at his marriage coming to an end? Why is he looking so good? What is wrong with me?*

Nitin mentioned that he had been trying to get in touch with Gautam but had been unable to get through. He queried whether she knew of any planned quizzes that week. It had, after all, been a while since he attended one. (*Oh, there, he is talking to you because he wants to know Gautam's whereabouts! He has no other motive. Poor guy, he must be looking for a break after all that sordid drama at home—oh wait, maybe he and his wife have reconciled. There, that must be it! He looks so happy and so relaxed after all …*)

The conversations, the one with Nitin and the one she was having with herself simultaneously, continued. Priya gave him the required information about an upcoming quiz in Noida on Sunday.

"How will you be going? Should I pick you up?"

*Pick me up? Did I hear that right? Why? Why would he want to do that? Idiot, there needn't be any other motive. He is a guy—they don't think, not with their brains at any rate. Answer his question!* Priya heard Tanya's screechy voice in her head as she found herself accepting his gracious offer.

It was after Nitin left that the full import of the situation sunk in. Gautam and Tanya were not expected till Sunday evening. She, meanwhile, had agreed to go to Noida for a quiz with Nitin (minus Gautam and Tanya). *Am I daft? Should I call it off? What can possibly happen? He is married for heaven's sake. But so what? It might be labelled as a boring business quiz. No, of course he would not pull me into his arms and kiss me senseless. But that would have been good too. Priya Kaushik. Focus. Deep breaths. Calm down.*

Looking for something to distract herself from that relen tless chain of thought, she spent the evening going through the list, shortlisting three guys who seemed okay on paper and in photographs. Tanya, of course, was consulted via WhatAapp.

P: How does he look?
T: Who is he?
P: Potential husband.
T: Why? Wait for me till I am back.
P: Not getting married, T. Shortlist only.
T: Umm, okay.
P: What you think?
T: Nose too large; hair too oily but okay.
P: Hmm.
T: Zodiac?
P: Virgo.
T: Nitpickers. Too clever. Reject
P: Huh? Silly reason.

This continued through the evening. Tanya kept rejecting all the guys for the silliest of reasons (*Where on earth does she think a Fawad Khan can be found among South Indian men? And what is wrong in the name Ramachandran—it is a perfectly acceptable name.* Priya was perplexed, as none of Priya's reasoning made any sense to her. Wasn't Tanya the one who had been previously pushing her to find a good man till last week? But here she was rejecting each one of them.

To put an end to her fantasy about a certain married man, who had resurfaced in her office again, she sent off her shortlisted names to her mother that very night. The sooner she starts meeting these men and interacting with them, the better it would be for her peace of mind. Or so she thought. When her mother called her the next day, excited at her daughter's sudden interest, and rattled off phone numbers and email addresses, Priya had a sinking feeling in her stomach. Why on earth was she subjecting herself to this arranged marriage business? Why did she even have to get married? Agreeing to see potential grooms was a knee-jerk reaction to avoid thinking about Nitin. What if one of these so-called dates were to be planned for the coming Sunday, so that she could come up with an excuse to not meet Nitin. Oh, but then he would probably feel bad? *Silly goose. You have fallen for a married man who has by now made up with his wife and is probably making his third baby with her. Good Lord!*

Whatever Priya's internal dialogues or apprehensions, the die had been cast. She would have to now meet these three men, one by one, if they were to call or email. She wouldn't be able to get away from that. To stick to her resolve of avoiding unwanted situations and people who could complicate matters further, she came up with a solution. She decided to ask Sushil for a transfer to the corporate office, a few streets away.

For her peace of mind, she listed down all the benefits in an Excel sheet:

a) Cafeteria had a more extensive menu.
b) Office was located in a quieter street, less polluted as well.
c) The extended e-learning team worked out of here.
d) And most importantly, there would be no Nitin.

The disadvantages were conveniently ignored. How many could those have been anyway? Priya had initially considered asking for a transfer to the Bengaluru office but the idea had been abandoned, thanks to Karthik again.

By Sunday morning, Priya had to come up with a Plan B —a desperate one at that. The plan was cooked up hurriedly when her mother called on Saturday asking whether she had heard from Sridhar or Arvind (two of the potential grooms). The third one, Ramachandran, had apparently politely turned her down; the man did not wish to marry a Delhi girl, one who wasn't even an engineer. Neither Sridhar nor Arvind had called or emailed. She wondered what would she do if this too wouldn't work out. Maybe, she could consider doing an MBA or an MS in Statistics, preferably from the US or Canada! But truth be told, she didn't even want to study anymore. However, there seemed to be some benefits to it, like better job, better pay, and who knew, she might even meet the love of her life—an unmarried man for a change. Now the more she thought about it, the more it made sense. One must always have goals and objectives to work towards, as doing so helps in keeping unwanted thoughts at bay. With this new-found zeal, Priya spent the night, the night before the quiz date—erm quiz *day*—researching a bit about potential schools, their programmes and their requirements.

In short, Priya had yet another sleepless night and was looking pale, tired and jumpy, something that Nitin noticed when he came to pick her up the next day. He, on the contrary, was looking fresh and fine. The season felt like spring, every morning dewy, bringing with it a renewed vigour. All was indeed right with the world—Nitin's world at least. The poet in him (the one that had been buried following an earlier break-up) had been resurrected! Dreams of a blissful future, with the beautiful girl in front of him, took centre stage and became his main focus.

Priya sensed there was something different with Nitin that morning. Was he looking different? Unlike most women, who can easily sense any change in the person they are interested in, Priya was blissfully unaware. But, despite her daftness, she knew that there was something different in the air. It just felt different, lighter and livelier. *He* was looking differently at *her*. She was suddenly conscious of her appearance; was there a stain on her dress; or was it something on her face that he was looking at? Nitin was indeed looking differently at her As Lord Byron took over his mind and heart:

She walks in beauty, like the night;
Of cloudless climes and starry skies.

The only little hiccup being that there was nothing starry about the smog-filled skies of Delhi-NCR, for the sun was glaring, and there was dust all over, setting Priya off into a sneezing bout and triggering a conversation on the air quality. By the end of the car ride, they had explored solutions to the problem of pollution in Delhi-NCR, also listing out the pros and cons of living in other cities, and gushed at length about their love for Bengaluru. They were just about to dissect the problems confronted by modern-day Bengaluru when they reached the venue. On their way, Priya's enthusiasm for her Plan B about pursuing another degree had increased manifold. She also did not want to marry any Sridhar or Arvind or whoever. She did not even want to meet them.

The quiz was a success—even without them achieving any ranking. With work keeping him busy, Gautam was not around much lately. Due to this, there had been some doubts about their participation, something both were fully aware of when they set off to Noida. Priya had checked with Vishal about his availability for the quiz. However, much to Nitin's relief, Vishal had a prior engagement and couldn't make it. Some other names were also tossed around but to no avail. Taking a huge chance, and also grabbing the opportunity to spend time with the other (something Priya would not admit even to herself), they reached the venue, not sure whether they would even be able to participate.

Nitin was in for a disappointment. His hopes of turning the day into a movie-lunch date instead were dashed when they found a teammate. But, for Priya, it came as a huge relief, as she had been battling with the butterflies in her stomach, thinking what would have happened had they not found one! Her Bollywood fanatic mind had drawn up many fantasies of what could happen if the hero and heroine were left stranded somewhere ...

They did stop for a quick bite on the way back to GK and Gurugram, but that could hardly be counted as a date—or could it be? As they waited for their food to be served, and lively conversation resumed, it seemed like there was magic in the air. The quaint ambience of the cosy Italian restaurant and the smell of freshly baked bread added to the vibe. Common interests and passions were discovered, Bengaluru roads and infrastructure animatedly dissected, and an unspoken bond formed ... Or so it seemed to Nitin. As he watched her speak, eyes flashing bright, and her hair falling on her forehead, he was lapsing into his poetic self. And since he wouldn't just be content comparing his beloved to a lovely summer's day—which that particular day had most certainly been—he needed to get his act together. For one, he was curious to know about her exact relationship status with Vishal. He knew he couldn't bring in such a personal topic into the conversation out of the blue. It wasn't as if he had shared many personal details either—barring a reference to his parents and one odd reference to his exasperating sister.

As he pondered, not too sure, on how to tilt the conversation in that direction, Priya's phone beeped. Seeing the number and name, Priya started. Excusing herself, she walked out, spoke for what seemed an eternity, and came back looking rather lost.

"Was that Vishal?" asked Nitin, the green-eyed monster rearing its ugly head.

She looked surprised at the question. "No, why would he call? Besides, it is a Sunday ..." Realizing that she was probably looking too distracted, she apologized. With the comfort of the cosy environment taking over once again, she started speaking. Her parents were looking for a match for her. The caller was a prospective groom, Sridhar, from Bengaluru. He was planning to be in Delhi later that week and wanted to meet her in person. And that was it.

For a second, Nitin did not know how to respond. "What about Vishal?" was all he could manage.

Priya looked at him, wondering whether he had lost his mind. Here she was telling him about a guy she may end up marrying and he was asking about Vishal! Was *he in love* with Vishal?! Was that why his wife had walked out on him? She hesitantly asked him why was he so curious about Vishal after all?

"Were you guys not dating?"

"What?!" Priya was horrified. Of course, she was not dating Vishal or anyone. She was in the arranged marriage market.

Nitin felt elated at this admission. Vishal Ganotra was not her boyfriend. As for the Sridhars of the world, he could handle them all. His job was cut out for him. He needed to speak with his parents, inform them about Priya, and then formally offer his hand in marriage. Priya certainly had no clue.

As the evening came to a close, this glorious summer day was to be remembered very differently by the two of them. For Nitin, the poet all set to turn a householder, it was the day when he had made up his mind to marry the girl of his dreams. For Priya, it was a day when her heart was broken into a million pieces; she could not stop mulling over her new conclusion—that Nitin was homosexual. Her heart went out to his poor wife.

# CHAPTER 17

And that is the state in which Tanya was to find Priya, all heartbroken and despondent, when she came back later that night from Amritsar, excited and bursting with tales to share. The supposedly sad trip to attend a funeral had instead turned out to be a nice, long vacation with the family. With this trip, her relationshiop with Gautam, who also accompanied her, had strengthened further and formalized. Gautam's parents had also turned up from Dehradun to pay their respects to their would-be-daughter-in-law's departed grandaunt, and to solemnize this relationship. No sooner had the obligatory prayers been said for the departed soul, the grandaunt had been forgotten, relegated to a luminous photograph in a rich mahogany-brown frame, the Grovers got busy with their only daughter's upcoming engagement and wedding. Much had to be done—dates had to be fixed, locations finalized, trousseau and jewellery made, and guests informed. Tanya, living in her own world, was of course oblivious to these real-life concerns. She was currently bothered about the exact shade of her wedding lehenga, a topic that came up in each of her conversations with any and everyone—should it be red at all? Is that too passé? But if red, what shade of red should it be? What is the in-colour for the current season?

In all this excitement, the chances of her remembering the complete and utter mess she had created was naturally forgotten. In her defence, not much damage was done. She had also confessed to Gautam about her role in the Sowmya–Bharat mess, not mentioning how she had maligned poor Nitin's image, who after all, might just be a decent guy, despite having a penchant for starring in not-so-decent ads. Gautam listened, horrified at his would-be-wife's antics. He wondered whether the next few decades would be spent in controlling this seemingly crazy woman he had chosen to be his mate? Well, any less besotted man may have acted upon these worries, but Gautam wasn't one of them.

So here was Tanya, back in GK, bubbling with excitement to tell her dear bestfriend all about what she had missed. But then she saw Priya, downcast and serious, scrolling through some Sridhar's Facebook profile. And then Tanya remembered. She definitely owed it to Priya to tell her about her complicity in this Nitin–Sowmya–Bharat mess. Tanya had expressly shooed Nitin away and called him names and actively dissuaded Priya from showing any interest in that man. Had it not been for her encouragement, Priya would not have agreed to see all these sad-looking men. This Sridhar, whose profile Priya was going through, seemed okay—not necessarily handsome but not bad either. Nitin did look much better. And now Tanya was in a fix. How could she ask Priya to stop focusing on these Sridhars of the world and instead choose Nitin. She feared Priya would flip and, worse, never ever forgive her for what she did. What could Tanya possibly do now to salvage the situation?

To her credit, she did try telling Priya a couple of times by bringing Nitin's name in the conversation, but Priya didn't pick up the hint—it did not look like she wanted to speak about Nitin. Tanya was now worried. Had she scuttled her friend's chance at true love? And what if, in this dejected state, her friend went back to that jerk Karthik, who once again seemed to have come back to India to lure innocent girls with his devilish charm? All this didn't augur well at all.

The competition seemed to be between this Sridhar (whom Priya seemed to want as her future husband) and Nitin (whom Tanya wanted for Priya as Priya's future husband). Now this Sridhar, based on Facebook and LinkedIn profiles, looked perfectly okay. Tanya couldn't help but feel sceptical about whether Sridhar really was who he said he was. What if he was a sheer fraud? Maybe she should get Dhamija to do a quick background check on Sridhar? That would be the right thing to do. Nitin had been subjected to one such check and had come out looking flawless, in the end. For the sake of fairplay and justice, she decided that that Dhamija should definitely investigate Sridhar's background. As she delved further, she was convinced that Nitin deserved a second chance at staking a claim to win Priya's heart and hand, and since Tanya herself was the one who had been the roadblock, it was now up to her to set it right. And then once a level playing ground was established, based on her efforts, may the best man win. After deliberating over her friend's situation, amidst excited conferences with family about the colour of her lehenga and the style of her blouse, Tanya decided to meet Sowmya and speak to her. Had she not indicated a certain amount of interest in Priya when they had last met at Dhamija's office?

Meanwhile, much was unfolding in the lives of the Ranganathans. Now that Sowmya's personal mess had been completely resolved and she had no pending domestic issues either—especially considering that Monju seemed to be sticking around—Sowmya's focus shifted back to her brother. Dhamija and his useless team were yet to find out how the makers of the paan masala ad had got hold of Nitin's mugshot. Nirala-ji had called Sowmya, quite a few times, with newer proposals. Completely convinced that Nitin was the one who had been born to essay the role of the male protagonist in his to-be-made magnum opus, Nirala-ji was not one to give up easily. If anyone could convince Nitin, it was he himself. With the set purpose in mind, he tried to enlist Sowmya's assistance, with the hope that the good lady would help him. Nirala-ji even suggested that he could come over to meet the entire family to assure them that he too wanted the best for Nitin. The suggestion was, thankfully, immediately shot down by Sowmya. She did not want to risk the combined wrath of her family.

Latha happened to overhear one such telephonic conversation between Sowmya and Nirala-ji, and that horrified her. What were her children up to? Barely had the divorce drama settled down, now her son was to be an actor—that too in Bhojpuri films? That was when she decided to step in. The best way to divert her daughter from pursuing a madcap idea was to get her started on another.

What she did not know was that extraneous forces (read Tanya's meddling) had initiated the chaos, affecting her daughter's married life. Meanwhile, Tanya, in her new-found purpose to do good by her friend and get her hitched as soon as possible, had called up Dhamija first thing the next morning, requesting a meeting with him. Dhamija's first impulse upon hearing Tanya's voice was to turn down the meeting request, but better sense prevailed. Maintaining a network of healthy relationships was critical to his trade and reputation. Crazy that lady may be, she still would have to be entertained. By the end of the meeting, Dhamija was seriously questioning his own sanity at his decision of entertaining her. Barely had the commotion regarding the identity of one young man been sorted, Tanya now wanted to send him to unmask the identity of another gentleman, that too one who looked like an absolute *bakra*. Poor thing.

"Madam, who is this man now? Seems so innocent. Why are you after him?"

"Dhamija-ji, your work is to solve a case. Please stick to that."

"Madam, I am saying so for your well-being. It is not very wise that each month you pick up one poor man and go after him. Anyway, all I could do was help you understand this. Now tell me, where does this man stay? And what is it that you want to know about him?"

"He stays in Bengaluru. Please do a background check on him. Who is he, is he who he says he is, all of that …"

"Ma'am, you want me to go to Bengaluru. Sorry. My business is based in Delhi, Gurugram, Noida. Haan, sometimes Meerut also. But Bengaluru? Please find a local detective there."

"Arre, there is Sowmya-ji after all. Your associate? She is from Bengaluru. You can tell her. She can certainly help you, but Dhamija-ji, I trust you and only you."

Since Tanya showed no sense of relenting and was hell-bent on handing this case over to him, he accepted the assignment. Dhamija had no plans of involving Sowmya in this stupid assignment. He felt guilty at having played a part, unknowingly, in that drama that had almost wrecked her marriage.

Dhamija didn't tell Tanya that he had an extensive network of friends and informers all over the country. This case, if at all could be called one, was child's play for them. This fellow looked too innocent to be involved in anything nefarious; all Dhamija had to do was verify his details. He had had enough of Tanya and her meddling. He made a mental note to gently convey this to Gautam. Poor guy, he needed to be warned. As far as Dhamija knew, a crazy wife is known to drive a man to an early grave. That was not what Gautam deserved. *Kismat apni apni.* In a bid to get done with this assignment, Dhamija touched base with a trusted informer in Bengaluru and set him on the job.

After initiating this part of her detailed action plan, Tanya contacted Sowmya, who was actually quite surprised to hear from her. Over a cup of coffee, rather haltingly, Tanya told Sowmya everything she knew about Nitin and Priya. It was conveyed that Priya had started liking Nitin since the day she saw him in that ad. But then she saw Sowmya and the kids with him at the airport, and assumed Nitin was a married man. That was the end of it.

"Priya is a good girl, wonderful and lovely, and Nitin knows her too. And moreover, since Priya's parents are looking for an arranged match for her, won't it be good if Nitin was one of the grooms proposed?"

Sowmya listened to this intently and saw some sense in the suggestion. "You do make sense. From what I can make out, Priya is beautiful and Nitin seems to like her too. Wait, where did you say her parents live in Bengaluru?"

"Some place called Jayanagar?"

"Ah—Jayanagar—that is old Bengaluru—definitely a sign of good pedigree. Let me discuss this with my mother. If she can be persuaded to see some sense in this, then we have our work cut out. Nitin will just need to be presented as a candidate to Priya's folks and then to Priya."

"Of course this should work, provided Kaushik uncle and Sharada aunty agree. But then why would they not? This sounds good," averred Tanya.

Sowmya raised this topic with her mother that very evening over dinner. Latha was definitely interested, more so because all the checkboxes had been ticked—the girl seemed okay, the family seemed to be decent and from Bengaluru, and Nitin knew the girl. "It is definitely worth trying. I think I will speak to him over the next few days."

"Oh, no, Amma, don't. Telling him may just be counterproductive."

"But you just said he likes her."

"Yes, he does find her pretty but who knows whether he even wants to marry her. He may flatly refuse. And what if he opposes our other attempts after that."

"True. That silly boy is capable of doing that. Let me not raise the topic at all then," Latha surmised and the women decided to not speak to Nitin.

Instead they spoke to Ranganathan, who was busy with his set routine of temple visits, family, friends and plants, and apprised him of this grand plan. While he did not approve of keeping his son (out of the loop) with regard to such an important decision of his life, years of living with these two strong, self-willed women had taught him not to protest or worry too much. The women shall do what they shall do. Better to let things take their natural course, instead of interfering and causing new obstructions and confusions. A mild-mannered gentleman of a distinctly philosophical nature, Mr Ranganathan had learnt early in life to not harbour any expectations from anyone—be it family or friends. He believed in doing his duty without expecting any results in return. What was to happen would definitely happen, so he was content being an observer as life played out in front of his eyes, doing what was expected of him as a human being, husband and father. When informed about this candidate and asked to go and meet her parents, he was partly relieved. At least, he did not have to go out of Bengaluru (even though the commute from Malleshwaram to Jayanagar and back did feel like an outstation trip) to find a bride for his son. Mr Ranganathan thus called Mr Kaushik a day later. The phone call took Mr and Mrs Kaushik by complete surprise.

The previous evening, they had received a call from their daughter who was complaining about the whole arranged marriage circus. She had met Sridhar and later confirmed to her parents that she was hardly interested in him. She lamented about the personality of men from their community, most of whom were settled in India, and went ahead and told them about her future plans of pursuing an MBA or an MS or something of the kind. Sharada, the ever-practical lady, reminded her daughter that plans need work and follow-up if we want them to materialize. Considering that Priya usually spent most of her time at work and/or gallivanting around the city with Tanya, that silly friend of hers, she did not see much of her plans materializing in the near future. She added that if Priya was indeed serious about her MBA aspirations, it would do her good if she stayed home and prepared diligently. Poor Priya ended up feeling acutely chastised. The conversation with her parents came to an abrupt end. Not that Sharada was worried—there were other suitable men after all. Whoever was made for their daughter would come into her life eventually. She was sure about it—call it a mother's instinct. Therefore, when the call from Ranganathans came, the Kaushiks were pleasantly surprised and hopeful.

As for the meeting between Priya and Sridhar, things went wrong right from the beginning. Priya had got into a huge argument with her cab driver, who tried to fleece her out of her hard-earned money. And then when she reached the place where she was supposed to meet him for the coffee date, the man was not there yet. A by-product of a disciplined South Indian upbringing is that one becomes highly intolerant to unpunctuality. What she did not know was that Sridhar had got lost while trying to find his way in a city that he did not quite like. A man of set routines, a pucca Bengaluruan at that, Sridhar hated Delhi with all his heart. He would not have taken the trouble to come and meet Priya had it not been for an opportunity regarding a business trip. He had decided to club it with the "see-the-girl-routine", an activity he was pursuing only to please his parents. Left to himself, he would have married his college sweetheart long back but then that North Indian girl had run away with someone else, breaking his heart. Focusing on work since then, Sridhar wasn't too keen on marriage. But then, if he had to meet some woman all because his mother had asked him to, he would. He arrived, late and irritated, not caring to impress. Peeved at being made to wait, Priya was neither friendly nor warm. And plus, this man was hardly like Nitin—no, not just in the looks department but also in terms of deportment and personality.

Sridhar also had a fixed picture of the type of woman he would eventually marry—docile, nice and sweet—certainly not like the sulking, scowling girl in front of him. So, before long, both of them were eager to call it off and go back to their respective homes.

Priya was done meeting strange men. If it was her destiny to fall for a married man (on top of that, one who was gay), so be it. There was no point fighting it. Instead of obsessing over that, it would be better to pursue her MBA instead, she thought. She came back home and cribbed to her parents and Tanya about the disastrous date, blasting that Sridhar chap, and of course cursing Karthik. Had he not shown up, divorced, and asked about her, she would never have agreed to this madness. Tanya was happy that the Sridhar date turned out to be a dud. Sowmya had duly updated her about the latest developments regarding their action plan, which was now finally on the right track. Tanya went to bed, that night, still undecided about the colour of the lehenga, but happy that nothing could go wrong in her friend's budding love story. Priya would get the man of her dreams, who may be a lowbrow model, but thankfully a *single* lowbrow model.

# CHAPTER 18

Priya, who obviously was not privy to any of these background developments, was not at peace when she went to bed that night. In fact, she woke up tired, bleary-eyed and cranky the next morning. Dragging herself to office, she managed to get through a part of what was turning out to be a calamitous day. Sushil was in one of those moods that he would get into after returning from his trip to Chicago. With the head of the corporate accounts e-learning team sitting out of a suburb in Chicago, Sharma would go there every few months to show his face to the big boss. A tall, large man with a clean-shaven round pate, Rajesh Batra, was known to be irascible in the Kintech circles. He was delivering great results every year, thus ensuring that his team kept expanding, even though he wasn't anyone's favourite. The team in the Gurugram office too dreaded these visits not because they'd sometimes have to go and put up with that man, but because Sushil would always come back in a foul mood. And as the day went on, his mood deteriorated, yelling increased and so did the workload of the people in the corporate accounts e-learning division.

In and out of difficult meetings, as she tried to deliver on all the impossible, urgent requirements, Priya was running around in circles, almost like a headless chicken, exclaiming to Vishal over lunch. *A charming headless chicken,* thought Nitin, as he walked into the corner where Priya was lunching with Vishal and the Parity Global team, not that she lunched with them daily.

She had learnt that Nitin was not expected at the KintechLearning office at all that day and she felt safe thinking that the coast was clear. But alas, the man made an appearance, sending her into all sorts of flutters. The previous evening had provided her with a moment of complete clarity—no one could compare with this man in question, and there was no point fighting the attraction anymore. She, however, intended to stay away from Nitin as far as possible. Idiot she may be, home-breaker, she certainly wasn't. If this was her resolve, Nitin's was exactly the opposite. He intended to spend as much time as he could with her.

It was therefore a pleasant surprise when he saw her in the Parity Global corner. He didn't need an excuse to go looking for her. Making his admiration and intentions rather obvious, Nitin sat down next to her, focusing on her as they ate, much to the amusement of Urvashi and Anuj. His team was convinced that it was just a matter of time before their boss would fall down on his knees and start serenading this young lady. What they were less sure about was her state of mind. She seemed to be blowing hot and cold—a feeling that he was also beginning to get as he sat that afternooon, staring at her, rather one too many times. At first, Priya was rather chuffed. Who would not like to be stared at, that too so adoringly and by the man of your dreams? The pleasant feeling soon turned into an agonizing frustration. Why was he looking at her like that? How could he? What was the point? Her mood plummeted further as she tried to ignore the blasted man.

If truth be told, Nitin was fascinated. Priya, he thought, looked very pretty in her blue outfit, which outlined her alluring figure. He was trying hard not to openly ogle at her straight back, her long legs and the way her hair, wavy and cascading, fell over her shapely derrière. *Do not look! No point in having uncomfortable thoughts during important meetings. Simply not done.* There was something fragile and delicate about her today, and he couldn't help feeling protective towards her. He wished to pull her in a hug, embalming, shielding her from the travails of the world. Such thoughts were aplenty as he watched her stoically get through a tiresome day. To other people, she merely came across as grumpy and plain irritated, but then they did not have Nitin's eyes, the eyes of a poet, the eyes of a man in love. As Nitin watched her through the day, the poet in him fully awakened, he felt like a bleak, 'unleafed tree' awaiting spring in Priya's absence. He longed for her love. Old, forgotten love ditties playing in his mind made him realize how incomplete he was without her. The sooner he goes and tells his parents (and her), the sooner shall he be complete. In short, what was a particularly exasperating day for Priya, was a magical one for Nitin.

By evening, Priya had fought with two designers, yelled at a couple of other programmers, and tackled two impatient clients. She looked forward to getting away from there. As she ran towards the elevator, something went into her eyes and her contact lens was about to pop out. Just what she needed to end the day! To top that, she had forgotten her lens solution at home. Rubbing her slightly watery eyes, mouth half-open to stifle a yawn, Priya entered the elevator and found Nitin inside. *Why was he in the elevator? He never took the elevator before—be it three floors or four, he always took the stairs. Why, had he not lectured her and some others just the other day about the benefits of going up and down stairs?* She did not refrain from asking him point-blank, thanks to her grumpy mood.

Nitin had taken the lift that day in the hope of seeing her before she left the building. The day was probably enchanted, for there she was, the woman occupying his mind and a frequent visitor in his dreams, entering the lift. She looked utterly charming, with her droopy, glazed eyes flashing brown and black, conveying a million thoughts, the half-open bud-like mouth, her lovely long fingers, as she smoothened her hair and rubbed her eyes. As he looked into her inviting, expressive eyes, he was lost. At that magical moment, where only the two of them existed, and the world had melted away, he pulled her straight into his arms and kissed her. Taken completely by surprise, all she could think of was how good it felt. What a toe-curling kiss it was! Sanity thankfully reasserted itself after a long minute, and the moment it did, she hurriedly pushed him away with all her might. *How dare he? How could he? What did he think he was doing? How could he be so shameless! What a perverse man! He was nothing but a lout and a jerk.*

The poor man, horrified by his own impulsive action and this mixed reaction, was rendered speechless. He had merely kissed her and was certain that she kissed him back, even though for a split second, before it all went topsy-turvy. Finding his voice, apologizing slowly, he told Priya that he had fallen in love with her, an admission that would send her into further paroxysms. More synoyms of the word 'shameless' were thrown at his face by a visibly upset and shaking Priya. Nitin was unable to fathom what could have brought about such outburst. It was a confession after all, maybe not as poetic or passionate as he would have liked it to be, but nevertheless a confession. Shameless, it certainly wasn't. Okay, he should have told her and then kissed her maybe? Is that what he should have done? As he thought more about his thoughtless, impulsive action, he felt idiotic, like a callow, immature youth who had messed up his case. How could he misread signals so badly?

As the day came to a close, sadly the magic had gone awry. Fairy tales do come to an end, don't they? This one, certainly, seemed to have come to an abrupt one. Nitin returned home, embarrassed, tired and unhappy at having seen his dreams crash down like a pack of cards. To mend his broken ego and to get a grip on his life, and not behave like some modern Devdas (again), Nitin decided to concentrate on work. He then decided to give his go-ahead for meeting one of those arranged matches that his mother and sister claimed to have lined up.

Nitin couldn't sleep that night, and come morning, he was off to Mumbai. A week away would do him a world of good and besides he wasn't really needed at the Kintech office.

While Nitin spent the evening planning his days ahead, following the disastrous end of his courtship period, Priya was fighting an internal battle of her own, completely miserable and heartbroken. *It does take a special kind of idiot to keep falling for entirely unsuitable men. That special kind of idiot has to be me. First it was that Karthik. But falling for Karthik was excusable, as those were teen hormones acting up. What excuse is there for this latest mess? I shouldn't have encouraged him in any way. Tanya is right—I should be supervised. I should be ashamed of myself ... but then why did he have to be such a good kisser! Damn you, Nitin. How on earth will I ever pick up the broken pieces of my heart and move on? How dare he think that I was so easily seducable? But wasn't he right? Oh God, he had seen through me—for the blathering, bumbling idiot that I really am. Damn you, Nitin!*

When Tanya came home, after a hectic day at Chandni Chowk, searching for just the right shade of red for her wedding lehenga, Priya was sitting on the couch, looking forlorn and hopelessly dejected, with a big bowl of ice cream and a bigger bowl of popcorn for company. Seeing Tanya, Priya burst into a long tearful tirade about how bad her day had been. She detailed all the fights, all the disagreements, Sushil's mood, impossible clients, but left out that one little bit that took the crown. Tanya consoled her by trying to find the right words to cheer her up. Maybe she should look for a new job. The idea was shot down, with the explanation that it was a comfortable job, the kind that one could even get married to! When every suggestion was rejected, Tanya got the message. Priya did not need solutions. All she needed was more ice cream and popcorn, and a comforting shoulder to cry on.

Thankfully, for Priya, the next morning came with a new set of challenges, ones that took her focus away from those of the previous day. Sushil's mood was getting worse by the minute and so was his yelling. With his expectations and orders changing practically every other minute, and the important deliverables due for the day, Priya did not have a minute to dwell about Nitin and the episode in the lift. To her relief, she found out through Urvashi that Nitin was off to Mumbai for an indefinite period of time. But this feeling was immediately replaced by a sinking one—a very apparent wave of sadness seemed to have overtaken her senses. Noticing her reaction to this news, speculation ran rife among the Parity Global team that something was wrong. Had their poor boss been dumped? Or worse, rejected? But wasn't he sitting around in the office the previous day, mooning over his lady love. And now he had disappeared. What could have happened? The team chuckled, knowing they had fodder for some gossip.

Nitin, in the meantime, had taken off to Mumbai, to clear his head, and mend his broken heart.  Of course, there were a couple of client meetings planned, but those were merely incidental. He just needed some time and space alone to banish the poet in him and become prosaic, practical and serious as before, and recover emotionally and mentally. With the practical man in him taking charge, he called his mother, before taking off to Mumbai, giving her explicit permission to proceed with the bride selection–elimination process. Nitin Ranganathan was ready to tie the knot, with any girl his mother and sister were to choose for him. Of course, the Ranganathan family was overjoyed.

The week thus went by, with the two heartbroken souls trying to navigate their lives, far away from each other. It was a burden tough to bear, with an uphill path ahead of them.

# CHAPTER 19

Unknown to Priya and Nitin, a chain of events had been set into motion that would help in mending their broken hearts. But for now, neither of them had any inkling.

Following the earlier brief call with the Kaushiks, wherein introductions had been made and the purpose stated loud and clear, an auspicious day was chosen for the two families to formally meet one another. In between, horoscopes had been shared, so that the respective family astrologers could look into those to their satisfaction. Once these minor details had been sorted and clarified, Mr Ranganathan travelled all the way for a day-long visit to Jayanagar, clubbing it with a long overdue visit to the Ragigudda Anjaneya Temple (second only to the Anjaneya Temple in Mahalakshmi Layout, as some would say).

The meeting between the two families went off smoothly. Distant relatives, common friends, and other similarities located, things augured well. The Kaushiks were pleasantly surprised to have found such a good boy (and family) with no effort whatsoever. Not wanting to jinx it or leave it to their stubborn daughter, whose whims and fancies these days were unpredictable, they decided that they would travel to Delhi the following week. The boy and girl could then formally meet each other (of course, they might have seen each other already, thanks to the same project they were working on), but it was decided that they should meet outside this professional set-up too, so that they could properly decide on the further course of action.

They fixed a date to meet in Delhi. Latha informed Nitin later that evening that he was to be in Delhi by the proposed date. They had found a girl they liked and wanted him to meet her. She would be coming over with her parents. He was also asked whether he would instead like to meet her elsewhere, maybe in a café? They even offered to forward her contact details to him. But Nitin was fine with the idea of simply meeting her at home with her parents. The impending meeting with some strange girl certainly made him uneasy. Considering he was the one who had given his parents the permission to carry on with their mission to marry him off, nothing could be done now. And it wasn't fair to unnecesessarily start talking to some girl when he had no intention of marrying her or anyone else for the time being.

When Priya was informed that her parents were coming to Delhi (and staying with Ranjini and Peri pa) later that week for a proposed meeting with some guy and his parents over the weekend, she was flabbergasted. Why on earth had they not told her before booking their tickets? Simply because they knew she would protest and scuttle any such opportunity. Priya protested and rather vehemently. Had she not made it clear after that Sridhar fellow that she wasn't interested. And who was it this time? Was it again someone from the list they had sent earlier? Sharada intervened just when it looked like Kaushik would agree to Priya's request. It was conveyed that they had never pressure her for anything before and wouldn't this time either. Acknowledging her preparations for GRE or GMAT—or whichever exam has caught her fancy for now—they asked her to reconsider their request, considering it was barely a matter of half an hour. This tactic of her parents always worked wonders, even when she was ten. And it also worked this time. Priya decided to carry on with this yet another painful visit and be done with it.

Before she could realize, it was weekend and it was time to go meet the guy and his family. On the way to the guy's sister's home in Gurugram, the meeting place, Priya reiterated to her parents that she was done with this farce. Never again should they force her or emotionally blackmail her into meeting another guy. Complaining, cribbing and scowling fiercely throughout the cab ride, she finally arrived in the gated community, situated close to the happening CyberHub. As the Kaushiks were let in by the security guards and reached the front door of the ninth-floor apartment, Priya stopped her rant. The door to the welcoming apartment was opened by a friendly-looking tall gentleman and soon they were seated. The friendly gentleman who went by the name Bharat Ramamohan was apparently the guy's sister's husband, or so they were told. Ranganathan, whom the Kaushiks had earlier met, entered along with his wife. They were delighted to meet the Kaushiks and were also happy to meet their daughter. She was indeed a fine-looking girl. True to her word, Priya bit back a biting reply and didn't say a word. She looked down, staring at her feet, planning a pedicure for the next day and deciding the colour of the nail paint. Why had the guy not shown his face by now? Well, some gentleman certainly did—Priya gathered herself as Ranganathan heartily welcomed him.

"Nitin, *vaa paa* (Come here). Meet my son, Nitin. Here are Mr and Mrs Kaushik and their daughter, Priya," said Mr Ranganathan.

Hearing the one name that she had tried to banish from her mind, Priya started. She looked up in horror, only to find Nitin looking equally perplexed. He too couldn't believe his eyes. Was this the girl his parents and sister had found for him? Brilliant! Seeing the colour of her face change from pink to red to purple, and her eyes flashing brimstone and fire, he had a horrifying vision. He could see her picking up the pretty red flower vase and flinging it at his head, while reprimanding him for his uncouth behaviour. He instinctively stepped back a couple of inches.

Priya, quickly recovering from her initial shock, turned to her parents. "This is the man you want me to get married to?" Priya asking such questions and that too in front of everyone did not augur well. Sharada was now worried. "He is a married man, and has two kids!" Priya blurted, rather loudly.

The Ranganathans were baffled.

"Who? Nitin? Married? To whom?" Latha was panicky. What had her son done now? Had he married a model?!

As for Nitin, he could not believe his eyes or ears. First, *she* shows up, looking rather regal and bored, and then starts accusing him of being a married man. Bloody hell. This was worse than having the vase flung at his head. Excellent, she thought of him as a characterless married man. He gave up and just plonked himself on the sofa.

"Nitin, what nonsense is this? Are you married?" asked Latha.

"Amma, no, of course not. Priya, may I know whom am I married to?" asked a peeved Nitin, in a sarcastic tone.

Priya looked up at being addressed and spluttered, "Err, I don't know her name."

"Ah, it's a *her*. Thank you for small mercies. And where can she be found?"

Priya, now getting even more bugged, snapped and told her parents that she wanted to go home and that they should run a background check before fixing up any more meetings.

Just as it seemed that the Kaushiks were about to walk out, leaving the Ranganathans in a state of utter confusion, Bharat, the ever-gracious host, intervened and asked the Kaushiks to stay back for a cup of coffee and some savouries. Since one never said no to a cup of hot piping filter coffee, the Kaushiks agreed and sat down. Priya, feeling rather humiliated at being paraded in front of him, who-should-have-been-forgotten, was aghast. She could not believe the shamelessness with which Nitin had shoved his wife and kids under the carpet. *Oh God, what a horrid man he must be. Look at him now, looking so peeved, as if he were the wronged party. Seriously?!*

Leaving the Ranganathans and the Kaushiks to talk about the weather, Bharat had gone inside the kitchen to ask Sowmya to hurry up with the coffee. He told her about the changed circumstances and that the meeting was fast turning into a disaster. The girl was pretty, yes, but didn't seem inclined to marry Nitin. On the contrary, she accused Nitin of being married and having two kids. Bharat didn't think anything was to come of it. As Sowmya heard Bharat's tale, she knew it was time for her to clear the great misunderstanding. After sending Monju with a plate of some savouries and sweets, Sowmya went in, with coffee. Priya was extremely disconcerted upon seeing Sowmya. *What a brazen man this Nitin was. His wife was right there, serving coffee, and he was not bothered—but wait, didn't this Bharat mention that his wife was in the kitchen?! Which meant that this lady was not Nitin's wife! She was in fact his sister. Oh God, what have I done? Poor Nitin. He was interested in me and I shooed him away!*

"Hello, Priya, I am Sowmya, his sister, not his wife," smiled Sowmya, much to Nitin's astonishment and Priya's embarrassment.

Sowmya, calmly for a change, went on then to clear the misunderstanding in front of the astounded audience, comprising her parents, the hassled-looking Kaushiks and of course Priya and Nitin. She also confessed about her role in this little matchmaking attempt, and informed Priya about Tanya's role in it.

As the tale came to a close, Priya, feeling rather foolish, wanted to sink through the ground. Feeling miserable, she looked up at an amused-looking Nitin and said, "Sorry about the other day."

"Which day?"

Mortified and terribly embarrassed at this reply, Priya asked if she could speak separately with Nitin. The entire family then shooed them both to the terrace, where Priya apologized once again for hitting him the other day.

The now highly amused Nitin moved in a little closer, and whispered in her ear, "Is there any danger of that action being repeated, since I want to kiss you now?"

Giving her consent and proving that there was no such danger anymore, Priya put her arms around him and kissed him.

# EPILOGUE

Some years ago, during the hot months of May and June, a group from Bengaluru set out on a *chardham* pilgrimage to cover the four revered holy spots of Rameswaram, Puri, Dwarka and Badrinath. The tour group brought together many devout pilgrims of a certain age group who wished to visit these holy places before their lives ebbed away. And with this sole purpose, they braved the heat and dust to bravely undertake this month-long journey, travelling in various modes of transport. Among these middle-aged and elderly pilgrims, there was a young man named Nitin Ranganathan, who was accompanying his parents and two old grandaunts on this grand pan-India tour.

Recovering from a broken heart after his girlfriend had eloped with his best friend, and desperate to get away from his routine, this pilgrimage came as a godsend opportunity. While the group was on their way to Badrinath, the Volvo bus broke down in a sleepy old village in Karnaprayag tehsil in Uttarakhand. As the driver tried to get the bus up and running, the largely city-based crowd, wanting to explore the lush, pristine green surroundings, decided to get out and look around this quaint place. For some locals, the confluence of the Alaknanda and the Pindari rivers was the place where Karna used to worship the Sun god; and for others, this was where Lord Krishna cremated Karna. There was even a temple dedicated to Karna in this place.

As the group walked around visiting little known temples and shrines, they passed by a strange, small photo studio, owned by an enterprising young man, Dharampal, who had got back from Joshimath where he gained some computer skills. Photography, of course was self-taught. Once back, Dharampal set up his studio, clicking pictures of locals and visitors, young and old, and displayed them on his wall.

Utterly charmed by Dharampal, Nitin's two grandaunts decided to help his fledgling business. They not only got their pictures clicked with much enthusiasm and cheer but also asked Dharampal to print all the photographs from their cameras. Nitin was also roped in to pose for some pictures.

Among all the pictures displayed proudly on the wall of Dharampal's studio was one of these pictures of Nitin's. The picture had been glossed a bit, photoshopped *a lot* to occupy the prime spot on the wall.

And it was this picture that landed in the hands of yet another stranger who took one look at the good-looking man and felt that he would be a good choice for his then to-be launched paan masala brand. The man was Shri Devi Lal Chauhan, the founder-chairman of Raj Group, who unfortunately has departed for his heavenly abode since.

Nitin Ranganathan thus unknowingly and unwillingly became the face of Ramvati Shaukeen Paan Masala.

# ACKNOWLEDGEMENTS

In conversations and situations, story ideas take shape. Once upon a time, I looked down upon romcoms and never imagined myself writing one. Back in those days, Priyanka and I were ridiculing a recent show we had watched. One thing led to another, and to my horror, I started writing a romantic comedy and had a blast.

Pri, you have played an instrumental role in my journey as a writer and in helping me realise my dream. For this, I owe you one!

Every book has its destiny—this story first appeared on a digital platform. For a long time after its digital publication, Pri mentioned that this deserves a paperback version. Years after this had been relegated to my memory as well, it found a new home and a renewed life.

Shantanu Ray Chaudhuri, I am indebted to you for giving a new home to this book and believing in it. Thank you!

Sakschi Verma, thank you for adding value with your incisive comments and feedback.

I also would like to acknowledge the support of the entire Om Books International team—Ajay Mago, in particular, and everyone else involved in the production of this book.

A special thanks to Ananya Saha for her support and insights.

I am grateful to my close friends, Kanchana Banerjee, Liji Narayan, Harprit Kaur, Kanchan Gupta, Angel Sivan, Manisha Kalaver, Deepa Pant and Maithili Sinha for always having my back.

Last but not the least, I would like to express my gratitude for all the love and support of my parents, my sister, Malini, my brother, Srirangan, my son, Nigamanth, and my husband, Vinod. My utmost gratitude to my Guruji for his blessings always.

